A Blaze Of Possessiveness Roared Through Him, The Need To Stake His Claim, To Mark Her As His, Now And Forever.

He was aware of the fine tremors that shimmered through her, of the way his thigh fitted between hers and how the cradle of her hips rocked against him. The intoxicating scent and taste of her filled his senses.

He was aware of everything about her. Only her. The rest of the world receded.

He was so far gone, that he didn't care about control, about leashing it, about the fact that someone might walk back into the office and discover him alone with her, kissing her. There was just Tiffany…and him.

And she was going to marry him.

Only him.

Dear Reader,

Welcome back to the desert kingdom of Dhahara.

If you read *The Untamed Sheik* you would've gotten to know Shafir and would've met his brothers, Rafiq and Khalid. Part of the challenge I faced in this book was finding a heroine to match Rafiq. Megan was so popular with readers that I knew this heroine would have to be pretty unique.

So, for *Saved by the Sheikh!* I started off by searching for a name no one I knew owned. I came up with Tiffany. Hints of *Breakfast at Tiffany's*. The glamour of Tiffany's, the jeweler. I adored the softness and vulnerability the name also seems to possess. Utterly feminine and exquisitely beautiful.

Despite never having met a Tiffany in my life, within months of starting to write the story, I'd met three Tiffanys. The first was an aspiring writer who won a breakfast at the RWA Conference in Washington, D.C., with myself and author Abby Gaines. The second was Tiffany Clare—who by some coincidence I met a day or so later also in D.C.—and whose debut historical romance, *The Surrender of a Lady,* has recently been released. The third Tiffany has the most wonderful name of all: Tiffany Light. When I told her that her name, without question, belonged to a romance heroine, Tiffany told me that her middle initial is D…Tiffany D. Light. Naturally, I wished I'd thought that up myself!

It's moments like these that add so much fun and wonder to the world of being a writer. You never quite know what will happen next….

I hope you enjoy Tiffany and Rafiq's story. Right now I'm thinking about who I'm going to match Khalid up with… and that promises to be a whole lot of fun.

Happy reading!

Tessa Radley

TESSA RADLEY

SAVED BY
THE SHEIKH!

Silhouette®
Desire

Published by Silhouette Books
America's Publisher of Contemporary Romance

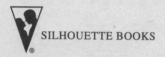 SILHOUETTE BOOKS

Recycling programs
for this product may
not exist in your area.

ISBN-13: 978-0-373-73058-2

SAVED BY THE SHEIKH!

Copyright © 2010 by Tessa Radley

Printed in U.S.A.

Books by Tessa Radley

Silhouette Desire

Black Widow Bride #1794
Rich Man's Revenge #1806
*The Kyriakos Virgin Bride #1822
*The Apollonides Mistress Scandal #1829
*The Desert Bride of Al Sayed #1835
Pride & a Pregnancy Secret #1849
†Mistaken Mistress #1901
†Spaniard's Seduction #1907
†Pregnancy Proposal #1914
†The Untamed Sheik #1933
Billion-Dollar Baby Bargain #1961
Millionaire Under the Mistletoe #1985
Falling for His Proper Mistress #2030
Saved by the Sheikh! #2045

*Billionaire Heirs
†The Saxon Brides

TESSA RADLEY

loves traveling, reading and watching the world around her. As a teen Tessa wanted to be an intrepid foreign correspondent. But after completing a bachelor of arts degree and marrying her sweetheart, she became fascinated by law and ended up studying further and practicing as an attorney in a city firm.

A six-month break traveling through Australia with her family reawoke the yen to write. And life as a writer suits her perfectly—traveling and reading count as research, and as for analyzing the world...well, she can think "what if?" all day long. When she's not reading, traveling or thinking about writing, she's spending time with her husband, her two sons or her zany and wonderful friends. You can contact Tessa through her Web site, www.tessaradley.com.

This is for the readers who wrote asking about the fate of Shafir's brothers, Rafiq and Khalid.

Rafiq's story is for you. Enjoy!

One

A male hand beckoned through the swirling silvery wisps generated by a smoke machine.

Tiffany Smith squinted and located Renate leaning against the white marble bar flanked by two men. Relief kicked in. The Hong Kong club was crowded—and a lot busier than Tiffany had expected. The harsh, beating music and flashing strobe lights had disoriented her. And the spike of vulnerability she had experienced in the aftermath of having her bag snatched yesterday with her passport, credit card, traveler's checks and cash returned full blast.

Picking up two cocktail menus, Tiffany headed through the mist for the trio. The older man was vaguely familiar. But it was the younger of the two men who watched her approach, his dark eyes cool, assessing—even critical. Tiffany switched her attention to him. He wore a dark formal suit and had a distant manner. Taking in the high cheekbones and bladed nose that gave his face an arrogant cast, she lifted her chin to stare boldly back at him.

"I'm not sure what Rafiq wants but Sir Julian would like a gin and tonic," Renate said, smiling at the older man who must have been at least three inches shorter than she. "And I'll have a champagne cocktail—the Hot Sex version."

Sir Julian. Of course! That would make him Sir Julian Carling, owner of Carling Hotels. If this was the kind of clientele Le Club attracted, tips would be good.

"Sure I can't get you something a little more adventurous?" *Expensive,* Tiffany appended silently as she passed the men the cocktail menus with her sweetest smile.

Not for the first time she thanked her lucky stars for the chance meeting with Renate when she'd checked into the hostel yesterday after her return from the police station and the embassy. Last night's accommodation had used up her last twenty Hong Kong dollars.

This morning Renate had generously shared her breakfast cereal with Tiffany and offered to bring her along to Le Club tonight to make some quick cash as a hostess serving drinks.

It had been Renate who had showed her where the trays of "champagne cocktails" were kept. Lemonade. *Cheap* lemonade. For the hostesses. Geared at getting the well-heeled patrons to order and imbibe more of the elaborate, expensive cocktails with outrageously sexy names for which Le Club was apparently famed—as well as billing them for the hostesses' over-priced lemonade cocktails. Tiffany had silenced her scruples. Renate had done her a favor. Anyway, Sir Julian seemed untroubled at the prospect of footing the bill for Renate's bogus champagne cocktails.

It was none of her business, Tiffany told herself. She

would keep her mouth shut and do as ordered. She was only here for the tips. For that she would smile until her face hurt. She glanced at the younger man, about to give him a glittering grin but his expression deterred her. His eyes were hooded, revealing none of his thoughts. Even in the crush of the club he seemed to create a ring of space around him. A no-go area.

She dismissed the thought as fanciful and forced a smile. "What can I get you to drink?"

"I'll stick with the gin and tonic." Sir Julian gave her a smile and passed back the cocktail menu.

"A Coca-Cola. Cold, please. With ice—if there's any that hasn't melted yet." The man Renate had called Rafiq curved his lips upward, lighting up the harsh features and giving him a devastating charm that had Tiffany catching her breath in surprise.

He was gorgeous.

"Sh-sure, I'll be right back," she stuttered.

"We'll be in one of the back booths," said Renate.

Tiffany found them easily enough a few minutes later. She handed Renate and Sir Julian their drinks before turning to the man seated on the other side of the booth.

Rafiq, Renate had called him. It suited him. Foreign. Exotic. Quintessentially male. Wordlessly Tiffany passed him the soda, and the ice he'd requested rattled against the glass.

"Thank you." He inclined his head.

For one wild moment Tiffany got the impression that she was expected to genuflect.

Renate leaned forward, breaking her train of thought. "Here."

Tiffany took the cell phone Renate offered, and gazed at the other woman in puzzlement. With two hands Renate mimicked taking a photo, and realization dawned. Tiffany studied the phone's settings. Easy enough. By the time Tiffany glanced up, Renate had draped herself over Sir Julian, so Tiffany raised the phone and clicked off a couple of shots.

At the flash, Sir Julian came to life, waving his hands in front of his face. "No photos."

"Sorry." Tiffany colored and fumbled with the phone.

"Are they deleted?" Rafiq's voice was sharp.

"Yes, yes." Tiffany shoved the phone behind the wide leather belt that cinched in her waist, vowing to check that the dratted images were gone the next time she went to get a round of drinks.

"Good girl." Sir Julian gave her an approving smile, and Tiffany breathed a little easier. She wasn't about to get fired before she'd even been paid.

"Sit down, Tiff, next to Rafiq."

The younger man sat opposite—alone—that ring of space clearly demarcated. Pity about the grim reserve, otherwise he would certainly have fitted the tall, dark and handsome label.

"Um…I think I'll go see if anyone else wants a cock-tail."

"Sit down, Tiffany." This time Renate's tone brooked no argument.

Tiffany threw a desperate look at the surrounding booths. Several of the hostesses Renate had introduced her to earlier sat talking to patrons, sipping sham champagne cocktails. No one looked like they needed assistance.

Giving in, Tiffany perched herself on the edge of the padded velvet beside Rafiq, and tried to convince herself that it was only the gloom back here in the booths that made him look so…disapproving. He had no reason to be looking down his nose at her.

"They should put brighter lights back here," Tiffany blurted out.

Rafiq raised a dark eyebrow. "Brighter lights? That would defeat the purpose."

Puzzled, Tiffany frowned at him. "What purpose?"

"To talk, of course." Renate's laugh was light and frothy. "No one talks when the lights are bright. It's too much like an interrogation room."

"I would've thought the music was too loud to talk." Tiffany fell silent. Now that she thought about it, it wasn't quite so loud back here.

Rafiq was studying her, and Tiffany moved restlessly under that intense scrutiny. "I'm going to get myself something to drink."

"Have a champagne cocktail—they're great." Renate raised her glass and downed it. "You can bring me another—and Sir Julian needs his gin and tonic topped up."

Rafiq's mouth kicked up at the side, giving him a sardonic, world-weary look.

He knew. Tiffany wasn't sure precisely *what* he knew. That the hostesses' drinks were fake? Or that the patrons would be billed full price for them? But something in his dark visage warned her to tread warily around him.

She edged out of the booth, away from those all-seeing eyes.

It was ten minutes before Tiffany could steel herself to return with a tray of drinks.

"What took so long?" Renate glanced up from where she was snuggled up against Sir Julian. "Jules is parched."

Jules?

Tiffany did a double take. In the time that she'd been gone Sir Julian Carling had become Jules? And Renate had become positively kittenish, curled up against the hotelier, all but purring. Tiffany slid back into the booth beside Rafiq and thanked the heavens for that wall of ice that surrounded him. No one would get close enough to cuddle this man.

"That surely can't be a champagne cocktail?" Rafiq commented.

She slid him a startled glance. Was he calling her on Le Club's shady ploy to overcharge patrons?

"It's water."

That expressive eyebrow lifted again. "So where's the Perrier bottle?"

"Water out of the tap." Although on second thought, perhaps it might've been more sensible to drink bottled water. "I'm thirsty."

"So you chose tap water?"

Was that disbelief in his voice? Tiffany swallowed, suddenly certain that this man was acutely aware of everything that happened around him.

"Why not champagne?"

She could hardly confess that she was reluctant to engage in the establishment's scam, so she replied evasively, "I don't drink champagne."

"You don't?" Rafiq sounded incredulous.

"I've never acquired the taste."

More accurately she'd lost the taste for the drink that her mother and father offered by the gallon in their society home. The headache it left her with came from the tension that invariably followed her parents' parties rather than the beverage itself.

An inexplicable wave of loneliness swamped her.

Those parties were a thing of the past....

Yesterday she'd tamped down the fury that had engulfed her after speaking to her mother, and called her father. To have him wire her some money—even though the thought of asking him for anything stuck in her throat—and to give him a roasting for what she'd learned from her mother.

This time he'd broken her mother's heart. He'd been tearing strips off that mutilated organ for years, but taking off with Imogen was different from the brief affairs. Imogen was no starlet with her eye on a bit part in a Taylor Smith film; Imogen had been her father's business manager for years.

Tiffany *liked* Imogen. She *trusted* Imogen. By running off with Imogen, her father had sunk to a new low in her estimation.

But Taylor Smith could not be found. No one knew where he—and Imogen—had gone. Holed up in a resort someplace, enjoying a faux honeymoon, no doubt. Tiffany had given up trying to reach her father.

"What else don't you like?" Rafiq's voice broke into her unpleasant thoughts. For the first time he was starting to look approachable—even amused.

What would he say if she responded that she didn't like arrogant men who thought they were God's gift to womankind?

The diamond-cutter gaze warned her against the reckless urge to put him down. Instead she gave him a fake smile and said in dulcet tones, "There's not much I don't like."

"I should have guessed." His mouth flattened, and without moving away, he managed to give the impression that he'd retreated onto another planet.

Had there been a subtle jibe in there somewhere that she'd missed? Tiffany took a sip of water and thought about what he might've construed from her careless words. *Not much that I don't like.* Perhaps she'd imagined the edge in his voice.

Across the booth Renate whispered something to Sir Julian, who laughed and pulled her onto his lap.

Conscious of the flush of embarrassment creeping over her cheeks, Tiffany slid a glance at Rafiq. He, too, was watching the antics of the other couple, his face tight.

What in heaven's name was Renate up to?

The rising heat resulting from the crush of bodies in Le Club and the sight of Renate wriggling all over Sir Julian compounded to make Tiffany feel…uncomfortable… unclean.

She downed the rest of the water. "I need the bathroom," she said in desperation.

In the relative safety of the bathroom, Tiffany opened the cold water tap. Cupping her hands, she allowed the cool water to pool between her palms. She bent her head and splashed her face. The door hissed open behind her.

"Don't." Renate's hand caught at hers. "You'll ruin your makeup."

"I'm hot." And starting to fear that she was way out of her depth.

"Now we'll have to do your face again." Renate sounded exasperated.

Tiffany held her hands up to ward Renate off. She didn't want another thick layer of foundation caked onto her skin. "It was too hot. My face doesn't matter. I'm not here to find a date," she said pointedly.

"But you need cash," Renate responded, her makeup bag already open on the vanity counter. "Jules says that Rafiq is a business acquaintance—he must have a fat wallet if he's associated with Jules."

"Fat wallet? You mean I should steal from him?"

Disbelief spiked in Tiffany. She turned to look at her newfound friend. Was Renate crazy? Tiffany was certain that Rafiq's retribution would be swift and relentless. She was feeling less and less comfortable about Renate's idea of easy money. "I could never do that."

Renate rolled her eyes. "Don't be dumb. I don't rip them off. You don't want to get arrested for theft. Especially not here."

"Certainly not here—or anywhere," Tiffany said with heartfelt fervor. As desperate as she was, the idea of a Hong Kong jail terrified her witless. "Yesterday's visit to the police station was more than enough."

She'd had her fill of bureaucracy after spending the entire day yesterday and most of today reporting the loss of her purse to the police, followed by hours queuing at the embassy, trying to secure a temporary passport… and a living allowance for the weekend. All hope of cash assistance from the embassy had been quashed once the official had realized who her father was. A father who was nowhere to be found.

On Monday a shiny new credit card would be couriered to her by her bank back home. And her temporary travel documents would be ready, too. For the first time since leaving home, Tiffany almost wished she had access to the allowance her father had cut off when she had chosen to do this trip with a friend against his wishes. What had started out as an exciting adventure was turning into a nightmare, costing much more than she'd ever dreamed.

But buying an air ticket home was Monday's worry. For now she only had to make it through the next two days.

Thank goodness for Renate.

Despite her sexual acrobatics in the booth, the other woman had saved Tiffany's skin by offering her this chance to earn some cash tonight. She owed her. "Renate, are you sure flirting with Sir Julian is a good idea? He's old enough to be your father."

"But he's rich."

Renate was fiddling in her purse, and Tiffany couldn't read her expression.

"That's what you want? A rich man? You think he'll marry you?" Concern made her say, "Oh, Renate, he's probably already married."

Renate drew out a lipstick tube and applied the glossy dark plum color then stood back to admire the dramatic effect against her pale skin and bleached-blond hair. "Of course he is."

"He is?" Shocked by Renate's nonchalance, Tiffany stared. "So why are you wasting your time on him?"

"He's a multimillionaire. Maybe even a billionaire. I recognized him the instant he arrived—he's been here before, but I've never gotten to—" Renate broke off and shot Tiffany a sidelong glance "—I never got to meet him. He's already promised to take me with him to the races later in the week."

Tiffany thought of the aching hurt she'd detected in her mother's voice yesterday when her mom had blurted out that Dad had taken off with Imogen.

"But what about his wife, Renate? How do you think she'll feel?"

Renate shrugged a careless shoulder. "She's probably too busy socializing with her country-club friends to notice. Tennis. Champagne breakfasts. Fancy fundraisers. Why should she care?"

Tiffany was prepared to stake her life on it that Sir Julian's wife did care. Speechlessly, she stared at Renate.

"The last girl he met here got a trip to Phuket and a wardrobe of designer dresses. I'd love that." She met Tiffany's appalled gaze in the mirror. "Don't knock it—maybe Rafiq is a millionaire, too. He might be worth cultivating."

Cultivating? An image of Rafiq's disdainful expression flashed before Tiffany's vision. He was so not her type. Too remote. Too arrogant. And way too full of his own importance. She didn't need a gazillionaire, much less one who had a wife tucked back in a desert somewhere.

All she wanted was someone normal. Ordinary. A man with whom she could be herself—no facades, no pretence. Just Tiffany. Someone who would learn to love her without drama and histrionics. Someone with a family that was real…not dysfunctional.

"Tiff, you need money." Renate flashed a sly look over her shoulder as she turned away to a soap dispenser set against the tiled wall. "What could be wrong with getting to know Rafiq a little better?"

Getting to know Rafiq a little better? Could Renate possibly mean that in the sense it had come across? Surely not.

"Here." Renate pressed something into her palm.

Tiffany glanced down—and despite the cloying heat, she turned cold. "What in heaven's name do I need a condom for?"

But she knew, even as Renate flipped back her short blond hair and laughed. "Tiffany, Tiffany. You can't be that innocent. Look at you. Big velvety eyes, peachy skin, long legs. You're gorgeous. And I'll bet Rafiq is very, very aware of it."

"I couldn't—"

Renate took both her hands, and brought her face up against Tiffany's. "Honey, listen to me. The quickest way to make some cash is to be as nice to Rafiq as he wants. You'll be well rewarded. He's a man—a rich one judging by that handmade thousand-dollar suit. He came here, to Le Club, tonight. He knows the score."

Horror surged through Tiffany. "What are you saying?"

"The men who come to Le Club are looking for a companion for the night. The whole night."

"Oh, God, no." She wrenched her hands free from Renate's hold and covered her face. The clues had been there lurking under what she'd seen as Renate's friendliness. *You can borrow my minidress, Tiff, it does great things for your legs. Your mouth is so sexy, a red lipstick will bring out the pout. Be nice, Tiff—you'll get more tips.* How had she missed them?

Stupid!

She'd been so grateful for what she'd seen as Renate's friendship…her help.…

Tiffany dropped her hands away from her face.

Renate's features softened a trifle. "Tiff, the first time is the worst. It'll be easier next time."

"Next time?" She felt absolutely and utterly chilled. And infinitely wiser than she had been even an hour ago. Renate was no well-meaning friend; she'd misled Tiffany. Purposefully. A sense of betrayal spread through her.

"There won't be a next time." Tiffany had no intention of ever setting a foot back in this place.

Renate picked Tiffany's tiny beaded purse off the vanity slab and slid the condom inside. "Don't be so sure."

Tiffany snatched her purse up and looped the strap around her wrist. "I'm leaving."

"First shift ends at ten," Renate pointed out. "If you leave before that, you won't get paid for the hours you've worked. Work another shift and you'll earn even more."

Tiffany glanced at her watch. Nine-thirty. She had to last another thirty minutes. She needed that cash to pay for her bed at the hostel. But another shift was more than she could manage. She met Renate's gaze. "I'll wait it out."

"Think about what I said. It's no big deal after the first time—I promise." For a moment something suspiciously akin to vulnerability glimmered in Renate's eyes. "Everyone does it—there's a lot of demand for young foreign female tourists." Renate shrugged one shoulder. "Rafiq is good-looking. It won't be too bad. Would you rather be broke and desperate?"

"Yes!" Tiffany shivered. Rafiq's disdain suddenly made sense. He thought—

Her hand froze on the door handle.

God. Surely he didn't intend... No, he hadn't even exhibited any interest in her. She'd only served him a drink—there'd been no hint of anything more. "At least Rafiq isn't expecting to sleep with me."

"Of course he is." The look Renate gave her was full of superiority. "Although sleeping will have little to do with it—and he will undoubtedly pay well."

The chill that had been spreading through Tiffany froze into a solid block of ice. It took effort to release the door handle she was clutching. "I'd rather starve!"

"You won't starve—not if you do what he wants."

"No!" Tiffany clenched her fists, a steely determination filling her. "And I won't starve, either." She'd foolishly trusted Renate. But she intended to make the best of the situation. "I'm only a waitress tonight—and he still owes me a tip."

Right now that tip meant tomorrow's food, and when she walked out of there at ten o'clock with her shift money, it would be with a generous tip, too.

Rafiq found himself blocking out Julian Carling's overloud voice as he focused on the archway to the right side of the bar where Tiffany and Renate had reappeared.

Tiffany wasn't the kind of woman Rafiq would ever

have expected to meet at a place like Le Club. Her face had a deceptive freshness…an innocence…at odds with the scarlet lipstick and the frilly, short black dress. He snorted in derision. It only went to show the ingenue act was exactly that—an act.

Yet as she neared the booth, Rafiq could've have sworn he saw her gulp.

She handed him a tall iced soda and stared at him with wary eyes.

"Thank you." Rafiq's body grew tight. He wasn't accustomed to evoking that kind of look on a woman's face. Usually there was admiration, a yearning for the worldly goods he could bestow. And a healthy dose of desire, too.

But Tiffany wore none of the too-familiar expressions.

Instead her pupils had dilated and transformed her eyes to dark holes in a face where her skin had lost its lotus-petal luminescence.

Apprehension. That's what it was. A touch of fear. As though someone had told her he trafficked in human beings—or worse.

He switched his narrowed gaze to Renate. Had *she* told Tiffany something to result in that pinched expression?

While the statuesque blonde had instantly identified Sir Julian, who was something of a celebrity in Hong Kong, much to Rafiq's relief she had not recognized him. Rafiq had wryly concluded that royal sheikhs didn't have the same cachet as hoteliers. In fact, he'd been ready to call it a night as soon as he'd realized what kind of a place Le Club was. One celebratory drink with Julian out of politeness to seal the first stages of the proposal they'd put together for a hotel in his home country of Dhahara, and he'd intended to leave.

Then Tiffany had chosen water over fake champagne cocktails and he'd been intrigued enough to want to find out what kind of game she was playing.

Flicking his gaze back to her, he took in the stiff way she held herself. Only the tilt of her chin showed something of the woman he'd glimpsed before, the woman who had demanded more light in this tacky made-for-seduction booth.

Rafiq intended to find out what had disturbed her. Shifting a little farther into the booth to give her space to sit, he patted the seat beside him. She ignored the velvet upholstered expanse, and fixed him with the same dazed stare of a rabbit confronted by a hunting hawk.

His frown deepened.

She swallowed, visibly uneasy.

"Sit down," he growled. "Contrary to popular opinion, I don't bite."

Her gaze skated away from his—and she blanched. He turned his head to see what had caused such an extreme reaction.

Renate was stroking a finger over Julian's fleshy lips and the hotelier was nibbling lasciviously at the pad of her thumb. Even as they watched, Sir Julian took it into his mouth and sucked it suggestively.

Rafiq compressed his lips into a tight line. Only yesterday he'd been invited to Sir Julian's home for dinner. The hotel magnate had proudly introduced his wife of almost three decades as the love of his life…and produced a daughter with whom he'd tried to match Rafiq.

"Nor do I devour thumbs," he murmured to Tiffany. To his surprise, relief lightened her eyes. Surely a sucked thumb was tame for a place like Le Club?

For the first time he saw that her eyes were brown with gold streaks. Until now it had been her hair and peachy skin that had snagged his attention. Not that he'd been looking—he wasn't interested in a woman who earned her living the way Tiffany did.

Abruptly, he asked, "Why do you choose to work here?"

"Tonight is my first time. Renate brought me—she said it was a good place to make cash."

He withdrew imperceptibly at her confession. She'd come prepared to barter her body for cash? "You want money so desperately?" When she failed to respond, disappointment filtered through him like hot desert sand winnowing through his fingers, until nothing remained save emptiness. "You should leave," he said.

A flush crept along her cheekbones. She looked down at the table and started to draw patterns on the white linen tablecloth with her index finger.

Rafiq looked away.

Across from them Julian's hand had weaseled its way under the neckline of Renate's dress, and Rafiq could see the ridges under the stretchy electric blue fabric where the other man's fingers groped at her rounded breasts. Renate giggled.

This was what Tiffany was contemplating?

"Will it be worth it?" he asked her.

She didn't answer.

He glanced down at her. Her attention was riveted on the couple on the other side of the table. She looked distinctly queasy.

"You'd let a man paw you for money?" He sounded harsher than he'd intended. "In front of a roomful of strangers?"

"I think I need the bathroom again."

She looked as if she were about to throw up as she bolted from the booth. Good. His deliberate crudity had shaken her. She'd said tonight was her first night. Maybe he could still talk sense into her. Perhaps there was still a chance to lure her away from such a recklessly destructive course of action.

His mouth tight with distaste, Rafiq threw a hundred-dollar note down on the table and rose to his feet to follow her.

Two

Rafiq was leaning against the wall when Tiffany emerged from the bathroom, his body lean and supple in the dark, well-fitting suit. He straightened and came toward her like a panther, sleek and sinuous.

Tiffany fervently hoped she wasn't the prey he intended hunting. There were dark qualities to this man that she had no wish to explore further.

"I'm going to call you a cab."

"Now?" Panic jostled her. "I can't leave. My shift isn't over yet."

"I'll tell whoever is in charge around here that you're leaving with me. No one will argue."

She assessed him. The hard eyes, the hawk-like features, the lean, whipcord strength. The way he had of appearing to own all the space around him. Yes, he was right. No one would argue with him.

Except her. "I'm not going anywhere with you."

Something flared in those unfathomable eyes. "I wasn't intending to take you anywhere...only to call for a cab."

"I can't afford one," she said bluntly.

"I'll pay for your damned cab."

Tiffany started to protest, and then hesitated. Why shouldn't he pay for her fare? He'd never coughed up the service tip she needed. Though the disquieting discussion with Renate had made it clear that tips in this place required more service than just a little company over drinks. Renate was clearly going to end up in Sir Julian's bed tonight. For what? A visit to the races tomorrow...and a wad of cash?

Tiffany had no intention of following suit. She'd rather have her self-respect.

Yet she couldn't afford to be too proud. She needed every cent she could lay her hands on. For food and accommodation until Monday. If Rafiq gave her the fare for a cab, she could sneak out the back while he was organizing it and hurry to her lodgings on foot. It wouldn't be dishonest, she assured herself. She'd earned the tip he'd never paid.

"Thanks." The word almost choked her.

He was suddenly—unexpectedly—close. Too close. Tiffany edged away and suppressed the impulse to tell him to stick his money. Reality set in. The cab fare, together with the miserly rate for tonight's work, which she'd be able to collect in less than ten minutes, meant she'd be able to pay for her accommodation and buy food for the weekend.

Relief swept through her.

All her problems would be solved.

Until Monday...

Over the weekend, she'd keep trying her father. Surely he'd check his e-mail, his phone messages, sooner or later? Of course, it would mean listening to him tell her he'd been right from the outset, that she wasn't taking care of herself in the big, bad world. But at least he'd advance her the money to rebook her flights and she'd be able to get back to help her mom.

"I'd appreciate it," she said, suddenly subdued. Tiffany halted, waiting for him produce his wallet.

"Let's go."

His hand came down on the small of her back and the contact electrified her. It was the humidity in the club, not his touch that had caused the flash of heat, she told herself as she tried to marshal her suddenly chaotic thoughts.

Her money.

"Wait—"

Before she could finish objecting he'd propelled her past the bar, through the spectacular mirrored lobby and out into the oppressive heat of the night. Of course there was a cab waiting. For a men like Rafiq there always were.

"Hang on—"

Ignoring her, Rafiq opened the door and ushered her in and all of the sudden he was overwhelming in the confined space.

"Where to?" he asked.

He'd never intended to hand her cash. And she hadn't had the opportunity to collect her earnings, either.

"I didn't get my money," she wailed. Then it struck her that he shouldn't be sitting next to her with his thigh pressed against hers. "You said you weren't coming with me."

"I changed my mind."

His smile didn't reach his midnight-dark eyes. Then he closed the door, dousing the interior light. Tiffany didn't know whether to be relieved or disturbed by the sudden cloak of darkness. So she scooted across the seat, out of his reach, trying to ignore his sheer, overwhelming physical presence by focusing on everything she'd been cheated of. Food. Lodgings. Survival.

She could *survive* without food until Monday. It wouldn't kill her. When she went back to the embassy she wouldn't let pride stop her begging for a handout for a meal. But she needed a roof over her head.

"I'm not going to be able to get that money back." She hadn't worked out her shift. "I doubt they'll take me back tomorrow now." There were strict rules about telling the management when you were leaving—and with whom. Tiffany had thought it was for the hostess's protection.

"You don't want to work there—find somewhere else." Rafiq murmured something to the cabdriver and the vehicle started to move.

Tiffany didn't bother to explain that she didn't have a visa to work in Hong Kong, that she'd only turned up at Le Club for the night as a casual waitress. Worry tugged at her stomach. "I *need* the money for those hours I spent there tonight."

"A pittance." he said dismissively.

Anger splintered through her. "It might be a pittance to you but it's *my* pittance. I worked for that money."

"And for what do you so desperately need cash? An overloaded credit card after frequenting the boutique stores at Harbor City's Ocean Terminal?"

His drawling cynicism made her want to smack him. Instead she tried to ignore him and huddled down into the corner as far away from him as she could get in the backseat. He was *so* overbearing. So certain that he was right about everything. Assuming she was a shopaholic airhead. Making decisions for her about where she should work, about when she should go home.

God help any woman silly enough to marry him—he'd

be a dictator. Maybe he was already married. The thought caused a bolt of shock.

What did she care whether he was married?

That fierce, dark gaze clashed with hers. "I'm waiting."

Trying frantically to regroup, she said, "For what?"

"For you to tell me why you're so desperate for money."

Tiffany cringed at the idea of telling him. "It makes me sound stupid."

He arched an eyebrow. "More stupid than working at Le Club?"

She supposed he was right. So she hauled in a deep breath and said reluctantly, "I was mugged yesterday morning. My passport was stolen *and* my credit cards *and* my cash."

It was mortifying. How many times had she been told to keep one card and a copy of her itinerary and travel insurance separate from the rest? How she wished she had. It would have saved a lot of grief. And a host of I-told-you-you-wouldn't-survive-alones from her father, when she finally managed to locate him.

"All that I had left was twenty Hong Kong dollars that I had in my pocket and I used that for last night's accommodation."

"How convenient."

The mocking note in his voice made it clear Mr. Arrogant Know-all thought she was lying.

"You don't believe me."

The seat gave as he shrugged. "It's hardly an original story. Although I prefer it to a fabricated tale about an ailing grandfather or a brother with leukemia."

He thought she was angling for sympathy. She stared

across the backseat in disbelief. "Good grief, but you're cynical. I hope I never become like you."

In the flash of passing lights she glimpsed a flare of emotion in his eyes. Then it vanished as darkness closed around them again. "And I hope, for your sake, that you are not as naive as you pretend to be."

"I'm not naive," Tiffany said, annoyed by the nerve he'd unwittingly struck. He sounded exactly like her father.

"Then come up with a better story."

"It's true. Do you think I'd voluntarily make myself look like such an airhead?"

"The helpless, stranded tourist might work on some."

She glared at him under the cover of night.

His voice dropped to a rasp. "Perhaps I'm the fool. I find myself actually considering this silly tale—against my better judgment."

"Well, thanks." Her tone dripped affront.

Unexpectedly he laughed aloud. "My pleasure."

The sound was warm and full of joy. The cab pulled up at a well-lit intersection and the handsome features were flooded with light. Tiffany caught her breath at the sudden, startling charm that warmed his face, and somewhere deep in the pit of her stomach liquid heat melted. For a heady fragment of time she almost allowed herself smile, too, and laugh at the ridiculousness of her plight.

Then she came to her senses.

"It's not funny," she said with more than a hint of rebellion.

Rafiq moved his weight on the seat beside her. "No, I don't suppose it would be—if your story were true."

Rafiq's brooding gaze settled on the woman bundled up against the door. If she moved any farther away from him, she'd be in serious danger of falling out. Was she telling the truth? Or was it all an elaborate charade?

The lights changed and the vehicle pulled away from the intersection. "Don't you have anyone you can borrow money from?"

She turned her head and looked out into the night. "No."

Frowning now, Rafiq stared at the dark shape of her head and pale curve of her cheek that was all he could see from this perspective, highlighted every few seconds by flashes from passing neon signs.

"What about your friend Renate? Can't she help you out?"

She gave a strangled laugh. "Hardly a friend. I only met her today. She lodges at the hostel I'm staying at."

Aah. He started to see the light. "There's no one else?"

She shook her head. "Not someone I can ask for money."

Rafiq waited for a heartbeat. For two. Then three. But the expected plea never came.

"You're traveling by yourself." It was a statement. And it explained so much, Rafiq decided, the reluctant urge to believe her growing stronger by the minute.

Tiffany shifted, and he sensed her uneasy glance before she turned back to the window.

She'd be a fool to tell him if she was. Or perhaps this was part of an act designed to make him feel more sympathy for a young woman all alone and out of her depth.

Had he been hustled by an expert? To Rafiq's disquiet he wasn't certain. And he was not accustomed to being rendered uncertain, off-balance. Particularly not by a woman. A young, attractive woman.

He was far from being an impressionable youth.

Three times he'd been in love. Three times he'd been on the brink of proposing marriage. And each time, much to his father's fury, he'd pulled away. At the last moment Rafiq had discovered that the desire, the sparkle, had burnt out under the weight of family expectation.

Rafiq himself didn't understand how something that started with so much hope and promise could fizzle out so disappointingly as soon as his father started to talk marriage settlements.

"So how much money do you need?" He directed the question to the sliver of sculpted cheek that was all he could see of her face.

This should establish whether he was being hustled.

A modest request for only a few dollars to cover necessities and shelter until she could arrange for her bank to put her back in funds would make it easier to swallow her tale.

"Enough to cover my bed and food until Monday."

Rafiq released the breath that he hadn't even been aware of holding.

As head of the Royal Bank of Dhahara he was familiar with all kinds of fraud, from the simplest ploys that emptied the pockets of soft-hearted elders to complex Internet frauds. Tiffany would not be seeing him again, so this was her only opportunity to try stripping him of a substantial amount of money and she had not taken it. She was in genuine need. All she wanted—and she hadn't even directly asked him for it yet—was a small amount of cash to tide her over.

This was not a scam.

The first whisper of real concern for the situation in which she found herself sounded inside his head. He had a cousin who was as close to him as a sister. He'd hate for Zara to be in the position that Tiffany was in, with no one to turn to for help. Rafiq knew he would make sure Tiffany would be looked after. "Tell me more."

"Except…" Her voice trailed away.

Every muscle in his body contracted as he tensed, praying that his instincts had not played him false.

"Except…*what?*" he prompted.

She averted her face. Even in the dark, he caught the movement as her pale fingers fiddled with the hem of the short, flirty dress. "I'm not sure that I'm going to have enough available on my credit card to pay for the changes to my flight."

"How much?"

Here it was. Rafiq forced his gaze up from the distraction of those fingers. She'd just hit him with the big sum—a drop in the ocean to him if she'd but known it—and he couldn't even see her face to read her eyes as his hopes that she was the real deal faded into oblivion. The tidal wave of anger that shook him was unexpected.

It shouldn't have mattered that she was a beautiful little schemer.

But it did.

Rafiq told himself it was because he wasn't often wrong about people, that he'd considered himself too wily to be taken in by a pretty face. *That* was why he was angry.…

Because of his own foolishness.

Not because he'd hoped against all odds—

She turned her head toward him, and her gaze connected with his in the murky darkness of the backseat. He almost convinced himself that he sensed real desperation in her glistening eyes.

Anger overpowered him. Damn her. She was good. So good, she belonged in Hollywood.

How nearly had she hooked him with her air of innocence and lonely despair?

And so much smarter than Renate. He would never have fallen for the platinum blonde's sexual promise of a one-night stand...but this woman... By Allah, he'd nearly bought everything she'd sold him. With her wide waif's eyes, her hesitant smile...she'd suckered him. Like Scheherazade, she was a consummate teller of tales.

Rage licked at his gut like hot flames. He was wise to her now.

He would not be deceived again.

No one made a fool of him. *No one*. And he hadn't fallen into her trap—he'd been fortunate enough to realize the truth before it was too late. No, not fortunate, he admitted, shamed. He'd almost been duped. A slip of a female had drawn him so close to the claws of her honeyed trap, and proven that he was not as wise as he liked to believe. He could still be taken in by a pair of heavily lashed eyes.

Tiffany had been a little too confident. The mistake she'd made had lain in her eagerness to reel him in too quickly.

"Where are we?"

The cab had slowed. Rafiq glanced away from her profile to the imposing marble facade lit up by pale gold light. "At my hotel."

"I never agreed to come here." Her voice was breathy, suddenly hesitant. Earlier he might have considered it uncertainty—even apprehension; now he knew it was nothing more than pretence.

"You never gave me any address when I asked." He opened his door and hid his anger behind a slow smile as he consciously summoned every reserve of charm he possessed. "Come, you will tell me your problems and I will buy you a drink, and perhaps I can find a way to help you."

This was the final test.

If she'd been telling him the truth, she would refuse. But if she was only after the money, she would interpret that smile as weakness, and she would accept.

Rafiq couldn't figure why it was so important to give her a last chance when she'd already revealed her true colors.

She hesitated for a fleeting moment and gave him a tremulous smile designed to melt the hardest heart. Just as he was about to surrender his cynicism, she followed him out of the cab.

The taste inside his mouth was decidedly bitter as she joined him on the sidewalk. Rafiq hadn't realized that he'd still had any illusions left to lose.

Inside the hotel, he headed for the bank of elevators. "There's an open pool deck upstairs that offers views over the city," he said over his shoulder as she hesitated.

Once in the elevator, Rafiq activated it with the key card to his presidential suite.

He brooded while he watched the floors light up as the car shot upward. A sweetly seductive fragrance surrounded him—a mix of fresh green notes and heady gardenia—and to his disgust his body stirred.

Rafiq told himself he wasn't going to take her up on what she was so clearly here for—he only wanted to see how far she was prepared to go.

Yet the urge to teach Tiffany a lesson she would never forget pressed down on him even as the sweet, intoxicating scent of her filled his nostrils. When the elevator finally came to rest, he placed his hand on the small of her back and gently ushered her out.

Balmy night air embraced Tiffany as she stepped through frosted-glass sliding doors into the intimate darkness of the hotel's deserted pool deck.

Overhead the moon hung in the sky, a perfectly shaped crescent, while far below the harbor gleamed like black satin beyond lights that sparkled like sprinklings of fairy dust.

Tiffany made for a group of chairs beside a surprisingly small pool, a row of lamps reflecting off the smooth surface like half a dozen full moons. She sank into a luxuriously padded armchair, nerve-rackingly conscious of the man who stood with his back to her, hands on hips, staring over the city...thinking God knew what. Because he was back in that remote space that he allowed no one else to inhabit.

When he wheeled about and shrugged off his suit jacket, her pulse leaped uncontrollably. He dropped into the chair beside her, and suddenly the air became thick and cloying.

"What would you like to drink?" he asked as a waiter appeared, as if that slice of time when he'd become so inaccessible had never been.

Tiffany rather fancied she needed a clear head. But she also had no intention of showing him how much he intimidated her. Her chin inched higher. "Vodka with lots of ice and orange." She'd sip it. Make it last.

Casting a somewhat mocking smile at her, Rafiq ordered Perrier for himself. And Tiffany wished she'd thought of that herself.

By some magic, the waiter was back in seconds with the drinks, and then Rafiq dismissed him.

She shivered as the sudden silence, the silken heat of the night and the sheer imposing presence of the man beside her all closed in on her senses. They were alone. How had this happened? He'd offered to buy her a drink...to lend a sympathetic ear. She'd imagined a busy bar and a little kindness.

Not this.

He turned his head. The trickle of awareness grew to a torrent as she fell into the enigmatic depths of his dark eyes.

Tiffany let out a deep breath that she'd been unaware of holding, and told herself that Rafiq was only a man. *A man.* Her father was a well-known film director. She'd met some of the most sought-after men in the world; men who graced covers of glitzy magazines and were featured on lists of women's most secret fantasy lovers. So why on earth was this one intimidating her?

The only explanation that made any sense was that losing her passport, her money, had stripped away the comfort of her identity and put her at a disadvantage. No longer her parents' pampered princess, she was struggling to survive...and the unexpected reversal had disoriented her.

Of course, it wasn't *him*. It had nothing to do with him. Or with the tantalizing air of reserve that invited her to crash through it.

This was about *her*.

About her confusion. It was easy to see how he had become appealing, an unexpected pillar of strength in a world gone crazy.

The rationality of the conclusion comforted her and allowed her to smile up at him with hastily mustered composure, to say in a carefully modulated tone, "I'm sorry, I've been so tied up in talking about me. What brings you to Hong Kong?"

His reply was terse. "Business."

"With Sir Julian?"

A slight nod was the only response she got. And a renewed blast of that do-not-intrude-any-further reserve that he was so good at displaying. He might as well have worn a great, big sign with ten-foot-high red letters that read Danger: Keep Out.

"Hotel business?"

"Why do you think that?"

Tiffany took a sip of her drink. It was deliciously sweet and cool. "Because he's famous for his hotels—are you trying to develop a resort?"

"Do I look like a developer?"

She took in the angled cheekbones starkly highlighted by the lamplight; his white shirt with dark stripes that stood out in the darkness; his fingers clenching the glass that he held. Even though he should've appeared relaxed sitting there, he hummed with tension.

"I'm not sure what a developer is supposed to look like. People are individuals. Not one size fits all."

He inspected her silently until she shifted. "What do you do, Tiffany? What are you doing in Hong Kong?"

"Uh…" She had no intention of confessing that she didn't do very much at all. She'd completed a degree in English literature and French…and found she still wasn't sure what she wanted to do with her life. Nor did she have any intention of telling him about her abortive trip with her school friend, Sally. About how Sally had hooked up with a guy and how Tiffany had felt like a third wheel in their developing romance. She'd already revealed far too much; she certainly didn't want Rafiq to know how naive she'd been. So she smiled brightly at him, took a sip of her drink and said casually, "Just traveling here and there."

"Your family approve of this carefree existence?"

She prickled. "My family knows that I can look after myself."

That was debatable. Tiffany doubted her father would ever believe she was capable of taking care of herself. Yet she also knew she had to tread carefully. She didn't want Rafiq to know quite how isolated she was right now.

"I've been keeping in close touch with them."

"By cell phone."

It was a statement. She didn't deny it, didn't tell him that her cell phone had been in the stolen purse. Or that she didn't even know where her father was right now. Or about her mother's emotional devastation. Far safer to let him believe that she was only a text away from communicating with her family.

"Why don't they send you money for the fare that you need?"

"They can't afford to."

It was true. Sort of. Tiffany thought about her mother's tears when she'd called her yesterday to arrange exactly that. Linda Smith née Canning had been a B-grade actress before her marriage to Taylor Smith; she hadn't worked for nearly two decades. The terms of her prenuptial agreement settled a house in Auckland on her, a far from liquid asset. It would take time to sell, and Mom needed her father's consent to borrow against it. In the meantime there were groceries to buy, staff to pay, bills for the hired house in L.A....and, according to her mother, not much money in the joint account. Add a husband who'd made sure he couldn't be found, and Linda's panic and distress had been palpable.

So, no, her mom was not in a position to help right now. She needed a lawyer—and Tiffany intended to arrange the best lawyer she could find as soon as she got back home. The more expensive, the better, she vowed darkly. Her father would pay those bills in due course.

But Rafiq wouldn't be interested in any of that.

"How did we get back to talking about me?" she asked. "I'm not terribly interesting."

"That's a matter of opinion." His voice was smoother than velvet.

Tiffany leaned a little closer and caught the glimmer of starlight in his dark eyes. A frisson of half fear, half anticipation feathered down her spine. She drew sharply back.

She must be mad....

Sucking in a breath, she blurted out, "Sir Julian was born in New Zealand. He owns a historic home in Auckland that often appears in lifestyle magazines." The change of subject seemed sudden, but at least it got them back onto neutral territory. "His father was English."

Unexpectedly, Rafiq didn't take the bait to find out more about his business acquaintance. "So you're from New Zealand? I couldn't place your accent."

"Because of my father's job, some of my schooling took place in the States, so that would make it even harder to identify." Her parents had relocated her from an Auckland all-girl school while they'd tried to juggle family life with her father's filming schedule. It had been awkward. Eventually, Tiffany and her mother had returned to live in Auckland. But her mother had frequently flown to Los Angeles to act as hostess for the lavish parties he threw at the opulent Malibu mansion he'd rented—and to keep an eye on her father. Tiffany had been seventeen the first time she'd read about her father's affairs in a gossip magazine. Like the final piece in a puzzle, it had completed a picture she hadn't even known was missing an essential part.

"Your father was in the military?"

She didn't want to talk about Taylor Smith. "No—but he traveled a lot."

"Ah, like a salesman or something?"

"Something like that." She took another sip of her drink

and set it down on a round glass-topped table. "What about you? Where do you live?"

He considered her. "I'm from Dhahara—it's a desert kingdom, near Oman."

"How fascinating!"

"Ah, you find me fascinating.…"

Tiffany stared at him.

Then she detected the wry mockery glinting in his eyes. "Not you!" She gave a gurgle of laughter and relaxed a little. "Where you live fascinates me."

"Now you break my heart."

"Are you flirting with me?" she asked suspiciously.

"If you must ask, then I must be losing my touch." He stretched out his long legs and loosened his tie.

The gesture brought her attention to his hands. In the reflected glow of the lamplight his fingers were lean and square-tipped, and dark against the white of his shirt. The gold of a signet ring winked in the light. His hand had stilled. Under his fingertips his heart would be beating like—

"You might not think I'm fascinating but most women think I'm charming," he murmured, his eyes half-closed, his mood indecipherable.

She reared back. Did he know what was happening to her? Why her pulse had gone crazy? "You? Charming?"

"Absolutely."

Tiffany swallowed. "Most women must be mad."

A glint entered his eyes. "You think so?"

Danger! Danger! She recklessly ignored the warning, too caught up in the surge of adrenalin that provoking him brought. "I know so."

"You don't believe I could be charming?" He smiled, his teeth startlingly white in the darkening night, and a bolt of metallic heat shot through Tiffany's belly.

"Never!" she said fiercely.

"Well then, I'll have to convince you otherwise."

He bent his head. Slowly, oh, far too slowly. Her heart started to pound. There was plenty of time for her to duck away, to smack his face as she'd earlier in the cab told herself he richly deserved. But she didn't. Instead she waited, holding her breath, watching his mouth—why hadn't she noticed how beautiful it was?—come closer and closer, until it finally settled on hers.

And then she sighed.

A soft whisper of sound.

He kissed with mastery. His lips pressed against hers, moving along the seam, playing…tantalizing, never demanding more than she was prepared to give. No other part of him touched her. After an age Tiffany let her lips part. He didn't take advantage. Instead he continued to taste her with playful kisses until she groaned in frustration.

He needed no further invitation. He plundered her mouth, hungrily seeking out secrets she hadn't known existed. Passion seized her. Quickly followed by a rush of hunger. His hand came up and cupped the back of her neck. The heat of his touch sent quivers along undiscovered nerve endings.

Tiffany swayed, eyes closed beneath the sensory onslaught.

At last, an eternity later, he lifted his head and gazed down at her with hooded eyes.

"So," he said with some satisfaction, his fingertips rubbing in soft circles against the sensitized nape of her neck, "you will agree that most women are right. You are charmed."

Tiffany reeled under the deluge of what could only be cool calculation.

"*I* think that you are the most arrogant and conceited *playboy*—" she spat that out "—I have ever met."

For an instant he stared at her, and she steeled herself for retaliation...of a sexual kind.

He threw his head back and laughed.

"Thank you," Rafiq said when he was finally through laughing, bowing his head with mock grace, his eyes still gleaming with hilarity. "I am honored."

And Tiffany wished with wild regret that she'd smacked his face until her hand stung while she'd had the chance. Through lips that still burned from his kiss, she said, "You don't charm me."

Three

His amusement instantly evaporated.

Rafiq suppressed the flare of annoyance and studied her dispassionately. Her hostility surprised him. He'd thought she'd leap at the opportunity to seduce him. Had she gauged he was not easily swayed? Intrigued by the idea, he assessed her. Was the taunt a ploy to capture his attention? Was it possible that she'd known exactly who he was? Researched him?

He shook off the sudden concern.

No, she might be street-smart. But she was a nobody—an insignificant foreign girl illegally working in a dubious club in the backstreets of Hong Kong. He dismissed his apprehension.

"Don't look at me like that, you arrogant jerk."

No one talked to him like that. Certainly not a woman like her. With a growl he grabbed her hand and yanked her toward him. She made a little squeaking sound as she landed in his lap. Rafiq softened his hold, stroking his fingers in long sweeps along her spine. Bending his head, he nuzzled the soft skin of her neck, murmuring sweet words. Her gasp quickly turned to a moan of delight. He marshaled every seductive trick he knew. She responded like a moonflower opening, overwhelming him with her sweet response.

Rafiq fought against the intoxicating pleasure her soft body unlocked. Told himself he was still in control. After all, he'd only teased her...flirted with her...*kissed* her to determine how far Tiffany was prepared to take this scam.

It was a test.

He told himself she'd failed. Dismally. Even as she'd kissed him like angel. He should've been thrilled he'd been proved right.

Instead he drowned in her unresisting softness.

When she shoved at his chest, he blinked rapidly in surprise and shook his head to clear it. "What?"

She scrambled to her feet, her breathing unsteady, her eyes blazing. "You misled me. I didn't come here for this. I'm not so desperate for a place to sleep."

Before she could spin away, he caught her arm.

"Tiffany, wait. You insult both of us. You might think I'm a jerk but I never assumed you came with me to find a bed for the night." Although perhaps the possibility should've occurred to him.

There was something about her that made him want to believe she wasn't like that. Maybe it was her wide brown eyes that gave her such an air of sincerity. Or the baby-soft skin beneath his fingertips...

He brushed the observation aside. She was a woman—of course her skin was soft. It made her no different from a million other women.

Time to get rid of her, before she had him believing the tales she'd spun. He dropped her arm and drew his wallet from the back of his pants, flipping it open to extract a five-hundred-dollar bill. To his surprise his fingers still shook from the aftershocks of the kiss. "Here, this is your tip for serving me drinks—that should help cover your accommodation for a couple of nights." If indeed, that story was true.

Bowing her head, Tiffany mumbled, "I can't take that."

"Why not?" By Allah, she drove him mad. What did she want from him? "I always intended to give you something to tide you over."

Rafiq tried to figure out her agenda. He still wasn't sure what she was after. She was such a curious mix of sophistication and spontaneity. On the one hand she'd almost convinced him her purse and passport had been stolen and all she wanted was a few dollars for a couple of nights' budget accommodation. Hah, he was even ready to give it to her. In the next breath she'd told him she couldn't afford the airfare home, leaving him certain that he was being manipulated by an expert.

He couldn't work out whether she was simply a victim or extremely smart.

But his conscience wouldn't allow him to leave her homeless in case she really had been the victim of petty crime. He thought of his cousin Zara, of his brother's wife, Megan. What if it had been one of the women of his family in such a predicament? He would hope that someone would come to their aid.

"Take it, please."

She stared down at the note in his hand. "It's too much. After that kiss it would feel…wrong," she mumbled, her hair blocking him from seeing her face.

He couldn't help noticing the catch in her voice.

"Okay." Growing impatient with himself, for being so aware of the woman, he opened the billfold again and extracted a twenty and a ten before shoving the other note back. "Take this then—it's not as good a tip as you deserve, but at least you won't suspect my motives."

She tilted her head back and stared at him for a long moment. "Thank you for understanding."

Tears glimmered in her eyes.

"Oh, don't cry," he said roughly.

"I can't help it." She sniffed and wiped her fingers across her eyes. "I'm sorry for calling you a jerk."

Rafiq found himself smiling. She enchanted him, this woman whom he couldn't get a fix on. One minute he had her down as the cleverest schemer he'd ever met, the next she appeared as sweetly innocent as his cousin Zara.

She leaned forward. The scent of gardenias surrounded him. She rested her palm against his chest, her hand warm through the fine cotton of his shirt. Rafiq's breath caught in his throat.

But the hunger he felt for Tiffany bore no resemblance to the sisterly love he showered on Zara.

By the time Tiffany rose on tiptoes and pressed soft lips against his cheek, he was rigid with reaction.

"Thank you, you've saved my life."

She smelled so sweet, the body brushing against him so feminine, that Rafiq couldn't stop his arms from encircling her. He drew her up against him. "Oh, Tiffany, what am I supposed to make of you?"

"I'm not very complicated at all—what you see is what you get," she muttered against his shirt front.

He felt her smile against his thundering heart, heard her breath quicken as his arms tightened convulsively around her...and was lost.

* * *

A long time seemed to pass before Rafiq lifted his lips from hers.

As Tiffany's fingers crept up his shirt and hooked into his loosened tie, Rafiq forgot that he'd started this driven by perverse curiosity and affronted male pride, to see if Tiffany would kiss him when she'd vowed that she wasn't affected by his brand of charm.

It had all changed.

His tightly leashed control was in shreds.

All he could think about was tasting her again…and again.

Her fingers froze. "What are we doing?" She sounded as befuddled as he felt. "Anyone could walk in on us through those sliding doors."

"No." He shook his head. "That's not true. This private pool and deck are part of my suite—my key card activated the entry doors onto the deck."

Her breath caught—an audible sound. "Your suite? You said we'd have a drink…. I would never have entered your suite."

She'd withdrawn. Her eyes had grown dark and distrustful. Rafiq gathered she was making unfavorable assumptions about his motives. He couldn't blame her. "The bar downstairs is noisy—and full of inebriated men at this time of night. We wouldn't have been able to hear ourselves think." Much less talk.

"Oh…"

Unable to help himself he stroked a finger along the curve of her jaw. Soft curls trailed over the back of his hand. "You are very beautiful, do you know that?"

"Not beautiful." She sounded distracted.

He stilled his fingers, and cupped the side of her face.

Tilting it up, he looked down into her wide eyes. "Beautiful."

She shook her head. "Not me. Pretty, maybe, at a stretch. But in this light you wouldn't even be able to tell."

No one could call her vain. "My eyes are not the only senses attuned to you. I don't need bright intrusive light to remember that your eyes are the haunting tawny-brown shade of the desert sands streaked with the burnished gold of the setting sun. I don't need light to feel." Gently he rubbed her bottom lip with the pad of his thumb. "Your mouth is the crushed red of the satiny petals in the rose gardens of Qasr Al-Ward." His fingers explored her cheeks. "Your skin is softer than an almond blossom. Your cheekbones are carefully sculpted by a masterful hand to ensure that as you grow older you will only grow more beautiful."

Tiffany felt herself color.

A beat of time elapsed. Tiffany tried to summon the anger that had scorched her only a moment before when she'd discovered he'd brought her to his suite, but it had vanished. His touch, the heat of his lean body, the force of his soft words had overwhelmed her. She couldn't think of a single thing to say. She'd never met anyone remotely like him. He was way out her league.

Finally she gave up trying to understand the emotion that flooded her. Linking her fingers behind his neck, she pulled his mouth back to hers, his hair thick and silken under her fingers. His thigh moved against her hip, making her aware of the hard, muscled strength of him. When the kiss ended, Tiffany discovered that her heart was pounding.

Tilting her head back, she looked up into his face. His eyes glowed, he'd warmed, he was a long way from being the remote, distant stranger. A heady sense of being on a precipice of discovery overtook her.

Before she could speak, Rafiq grasped her hand. "Come."

He led her through a pair of French doors into a darkened room. A flick of a switch and dim lighting washed the room, revealing a king-size bed in a sumptuously decorated room.

Tiffany hesitated for a microsecond as Rafiq shrugged off his shirt. Then he turned her in his arms and the moment of cool analysis was gone.

Her wide, elasticized belt gave.... She heard something fall, and dismissed it. The zip on the back of her borrowed dress rasped down. His hands closed over the shoulder straps and eased them down her arms along with the tiny, dainty bag looped around her wrist. She didn't have any time to feel exposed...or naked. Only relief that the tight dress was gone. Rafiq drew her against his bare torso, his skin smooth and warm against hers.

His fingers tangled in her hair, before moving in small circles down her back, setting flame to each inch of flesh he massaged.

Tiffany flung her head back. A moan escaped. Desire flared uncontrollably within her and her nipples peaked beneath the modest black bra she wore. She didn't even feel Rafiq loosen the back before the plain bra gave and he removed it, tossing it over the bed end. Then he was on his knees in front of her, easing her heels off, sliding the cotton briefs down her legs, his touch trailing fire down the insides of her thighs.

She started to shake.

The explosive hunger that consumed her was unfamiliar. Powerful. Incredible. A new experience. He buried his face in her belly. Goose bumps broke out over her skin as sensation shook her to her soul. Her hands clutched at his hair, the texture rough as she closed her fingers over the short strands.

"I'm going to pleasure you—but we're not going to make love," he murmured.

Relief, instantly followed by a crazy kind of disappointment spread through her. "Why won't we make love?"

Did he think he was too good for her?

"I'm not…equipped."

"Equipped?" Then it struck her what he meant. "Oh."

The next thought was that if he didn't carry condoms around with him, then he didn't do casual sex, either. It made her almost start to like the man who had her in such a sweat.

Perversely, it made her want him to make love to her.

Tiffany reached for the puddle of her dress on the floor and found her bag. Opening it she extracted the condom that Renate had stuck in. "I only have one."

"Better than nothing," he growled.

Then he had her on the bed and everything started to move very fast. She closed her eyes as his mouth teased her nipple, arousing sensations she'd never experienced. A wild, keening sound broke from her throat as his teeth teased her burgeoning flesh. His hands were everywhere.… He knew exactly what to do to reduce her to a state of quivering arousal. Her body turned fluid. It seemed to know exactly what he wanted…how to respond to his every move.

When he finally moved over her, her legs parted. Opening her eyes, she glimpsed the tense line of his jaw, the fullness of a bottom lip softened by passion. He shifted into the space between her legs, his body so male, so unfamiliar against her own. He moved his hips, and Tiffany tensed, fighting the instinct to resist.

The pressure. Her breath caught in the back of her throat. He wasn't going to fit. Staring at the mouth that had wreaked so much pleasure, she waited uncertainly. Suddenly her body gave, and the pressure eased. The shudders subsided. Her heart expanded as he sank forward. A glow of warmth swept her. Her hands fluttered along the indent of his spine as a powerful, primal emotion swept her.

Tiffany thought she was going to cry with joy, at the beauty of it all.

The warmth spiraled into a fierce, desperate heat as he moved within her. As the friction built, she could feel herself straining to reach a place she'd never been. Her body tightened, no longer hers, taken over by the passion that ripped through her.

"Relax," he whispered in her ear. "Let it happen."

She didn't know what he was talking about. Yet the warmth of his breath against her ear caused a fresh wave of shivers to race up and down her spine, spreading out along every inch of her skin.

This time she didn't fight the sensation. She allowed it to sweep her away. Pleasure soared.

He grew still. Then he moved, his body driving in quick thrusts into hers, his breath fast.

A cry of shock caught in her throat as her body convulsed. Waves of heat broke, rippling through her, a tide of inexorable sensation that left her limp.

Tiffany opened her eyes and blinked against bright sunlight.

Disorientation was quickly followed by a suffocating sense of dread. *What had she done?* Slowly, she turned her head against the plump oversized pillow.

The space beside her in the giant king-size bed was

empty. Rafiq was already awake…and out of the bed. With any luck he'd stay closeted in the bathroom until she could escape. Except she could hear no sound. Perhaps he'd gone to have breakfast…a swim…to work out. Anything.

Tiffany didn't care so long as she didn't have to confront him.

A movement drew her gaze to the floor-to-ceiling windows where the drapes had already been thrown back. Squinting against the gauze-filtered sunlight, Tiffany made out the dark shadow of a backlit figure.

Rafiq.

She shifted and he must've heard the movement, because he wheeled around and spoke. "You're awake."

Too late to squeeze her eyelids shut and fake sleep.

"Yes." She offered him a tremulous smile, and tried to read his expression, but bright light behind him frustrated her attempt.

"Good."

Was it? She wasn't so sure. He moved closer and came into focus. The passionate lover from last night's dark, delicious world had vanished. Replaced by the aloof man she'd met—was it only the evening before?

Tiffany shuddered.

"You're already dressed." Did she have to sound so plaintive?

He shrugged. "I have a busy day planned."

And it was time for her to make herself scarce.

He didn't need to speak the words out loud. It was painfully obvious.

But she had no intention of getting out of bed with him standing less than three feet away. She was naked under the sheet. And he was impeccably, immaculately dressed. She'd exposed more of herself than she'd ever intended, and she had no one but herself to blame. He would not see another inch of her body. A fresh flush of humiliation scorched her at the memory of what had passed between them last night.

Tiffany raised her chin and bravely met his granite gaze. "So why are you still here?"

"I've been waiting for you to awaken."

The harsh features that had been aflame with desire last night had reverted to keep-out coldness. Any hope that he'd wanted to tell her something momentous withered. Her stomach balled into a tight knot.

"Why?"

He reached into his jacket pocket.

His fist uncurled. A cell phone lay there—slim and silent.

Tiffany frowned, trying to make sense of the tension that vibrated from him. And what it had to do with her. "That's Renate's phone. I slipped it into my belt—"

"You took pictures last night."

Oh. Darn. She'd forgotten all about that. "I meant to delete—"

"Yes." His mouth curled. It was not a nice smile. "I'm sure you meant to. But you didn't. And you assured Sir Julian that you already had deleted the images."

She'd been scared of losing her job—now she'd been caught in a lie. She wriggled under the sheet, trying to think of how to explain. In the end she decided she'd probably be better off remaining silent, before she dug herself into a deeper hole. What a mess.

"Nothing to say?"

"Why do you care?"

"Oh, I care." He brandished the phone at her. "One of the photos is of me with Sir Julian—and enough of Renate to make sure the viewer knows exactly what kind of relationship she's contemplating with him."

"I didn't mean—"

"Of course, you didn't." He sneered. "You were very interested in talking about Sir Julian Carling last night, too."

"I was making conversation." Tiffany was utterly bewildered by the turn the conversation had taken. "So what?"

His eyes darkened. "So what? That's all you have to say for yourself?"

Tiffany drew the top sheet more securely around herself. What had possessed her to let this daunting stranger get so close last night?

"You are wise to be nervous."

"I'm not nervous," she lied. "I'm confused."

The silence swelled. Tiffany *was* growing decidedly nervous. Her gaze flitted toward the door. Even if she made it out the room, she wouldn't get very far without any clothes. And she doubted she'd have time to scoop up her dress and bag off the floor.

She turned her attention back to him and decided to brazen it out. "Why are you angry?"

His eyebrow shot up. "You expect me to believe you don't know? Come, come, it's enough now."

Tiffany decided it would probably be better to say nothing. It would only enrage him further. So she waited.

"There's a text message from your friend on her phone asking how your night went."

The expression of distaste on his face told her that he'd jumped to the conclusion that she'd discussed sleeping with him with Renate.

Damn Renate. "You're misunderstanding—"

He held up a hand. "I don't want to hear it. How much do you want?"

"*What?*"

"To forget that you ever saw me with Sir Julian."

Her mouth dropped open. He was delusional. Or paranoid. Or maybe just plain crazy. That was enough to make her say hastily, "Just delete the images—it's what I meant to do last night. I forgot…and then I forgot to give the phone back to Renate."

"How convenient."

Tiffany didn't like the way he said that.

"When you didn't respond, your friend's texts make it clear she's decided you must've stolen her phone." He smiled, but his eyes still smoldered like hot coals. "That you're planning to sell the images yourself."

"I wouldn't do that!"

He made a sound that sounded suspiciously like a snort. "Sell the images or steal her phone? Since when is there honor among thieves?"

What on earth was he getting at? She gave him a wary glance, and then said, "Just say what you mean."

"You and your friend intended to blackmail me and Sir Julian. Your friend has decided you've decided to proceed alone. I think she's right."

"Blackmail?"

He was definitely, certifiably crazy. Her eyes flickered toward the door again. Maybe, just maybe she could get out of here…and if she yanked the sheet along, she'd have cover.

"You're not going anywhere," he growled and sat down on the bed, pinning her under the sheet that she'd been planning to escape in, wrapped around her like a toga.

"I know." She gazed at him limpidly.

His eyes narrowed to slits. "That look won't work. I know you're no innocent."

If he only knew.

"Uh…" Tiffany's voice trailed away. No point telling him, he wouldn't believe her.

"So what were the two of you intending to do with the photos?"

"Nothing."

He shook his head. "You take me for a fool. Your friend was desperate to know whether you still had the phone and the photos. Someone was ready to buy them. You were in on the deal."

She wasn't going to argue with him. Not while he was looming over her, and she wasn't wearing a stitch under the scanty cover that the hotel's silk sheet provided. No way was she risking sparking the tension between them into something else…something infinitely more dangerous.

Panic filled her. "Get off me!"

He didn't budge. "Here's what's going to happen. I'm going to delete the images from the phone. Then I'm going to buy you the ticket that you were so desperate for last night. Then I never want to see or hear from you again. Do you understand?"

Tiffany nodded.

He sat back and she breathed again.

"I'm not going to give you the money you so badly want. I'm going to take you to the airport and pay whatever it takes to get that ticket changed—so I hope you really need a flight to Auckland."

"I do," she croaked.

He pushed himself away from her. "It will be waiting for you downstairs when you are ready to leave."

As he rose from the bed, her bravado returned. Her chin lifted. "I don't need you to take me to the airport—it won't help. My temporary travel documents will only be ready on Monday. I'll take a cab back to the hostel."

"I want you out of Hong Kong."

"I have no intention of staying a minute more than I have to. Nor will I cause you any grief. I promise."

He gave her one of those narrow-eyed glances that chilled her to the bone. "If I learn that you have—"

"I'm not going to do anything. I swear. And, believe me, I intend to pay you back," she said fervently. Tiffany had no intention of being beholden to this man.

He waved a dismissive hand. "Please. Don't lie."

"I *will* repay you. But I'll need your bank details."

"To further scam me?" The bark of laughter he gave sounded ugly. His eyes bored into hers. She didn't look away. The mood changed, becoming hot and oppressive. Something arced between them, an emotion so intense, so powerful that she lost the ability to think.

Without looking away, Rafiq reached into his pocket for his wallet. This time he extracted a small white card. "Here are my details. You can post me a check…but I don't want to see you again. Ever."

It stung.

Determined to hurt him, she flung the words back at him. "I have no intention of seeing you again." Then, for good measure, she added defiantly, "Ever."

She bit her lip hard to stop it trembling as he swung away, and she watched him head for the door with long, raking strides. When the door thudded shut behind him, she glanced down at the card she held.

Rafiq Al Dhahara. President, Royal Bank of Dhahara.

She should've known. He wasn't any old banker. He was the boss. The man who had showed her a glimpse of heaven would never be an ordinary man.

Four

Rafiq could not settle.

He'd been restless for weeks now. He told himself it was the fierce desert heat of Dhahara that kept him awake deep into the heart of the night. Not even the arctic air-conditioning circulating through the main boardroom of the Royal Bank of Dhahara soothed him.

"Stop pacing," Shafir said from behind him. "You called us in to talk about the new hotel you've financed, but now you wear holes in that kelim. Sit down and talk." He tapped his gold pen against the legal pad in front of him. "I'm in a hurry."

Swiveling on his heel, Rafiq put his hands on narrow hips, and scowled down at where his brother lounged in the black leather chair, his white robes cascading about him. "You can wait, Shafir."

"I might, but Megan won't. My wife is determined to spend every free minute we have at Qasr Al-Ward." Shafir flashed him the wicked grin of a man well satisfied by that state of affairs. "Come for the weekend. Celebrate that the contracts for the new Carling Hotel are in place. It'll give you a chance to shed that suit for a couple of days."

Shaking his head, Rafiq said, "Too much else to do. I'll resist the call of the desert." He envied his brother the bond he had to Qasr Al-Ward, the desert palace that had been in the family for centuries. Since his marriage to Megan, Shafir had made Qasr Al-Ward their home.

"Don't resist it too long—or you may not find your way back."

"Why don't you take our father?" Rafiq wasn't eager to engage in the kind of analysis that Shafir's sharp gaze suggested was about to begin. In an effort to distract his brother, he tipped his head to where King Selim was intent on getting his point across to his firstborn son. The words "duty" and "marriage" drifted across the expanse of the boardroom table. "That way Khalid might get some peace, too."

Shafir chuckled. "Looks like our father is determined not to give him a break."

"You realize your marriage has only increased the pressure on Khalid?"

Stabbing a finger at his brother's chest, Shafir chuckled. "And on you. Everyone expected you to marry first, Rafiq. Unlike Khalid, your bride isn't Father's choice. And unlike me, women don't view you as already wed to the desert. You spent years abroad—you've had plenty of opportunity to fall in love."

"It wasn't so straightforward." Rafiq realized that was true. "There were no expectations on you, Shafir. No pressure. You've always done exactly what you want."

His brother had spent much of his life growing up in the desert; he'd been allowed rough edges, whereas

Rafiq had been groomed for a corporate role. Educated at Eton, followed by degrees at Cambridge and Harvard. There had been pressure to put thought and care into his choice of partner—someone who could bear scrutiny on an international stage. A trophy wife. A *powerful* trophy wife.

How could he explain how a relationship that started off as something special could deteriorate into nothing more than duty?

"Take it." His father's rising voice broke into his thoughts.

Rafiq refocused across the table. His father was trying to press a piece of paper into Khalid's hand. "All three of these women are suitable. Yasmin is a wealthy young woman who knows what you need in a wife."

"No!" Khalid's jaw was like rock.

"She's pretty, too." Shafir smirked.

"I don't want pretty," his eldest brother argued.

Pretty. Rafiq shied away from the word. Tiffany had thought she was pretty. Not beautiful. Pretty. Rafiq had considered her beautiful.

"I want a woman who will match me," Khalid was saying. "I don't care what she looks like. I need a partner... not a pinup."

"Hey, my wife is a partner," Shafir objected. "In my eyes she's a pinup, too."

Newly—and happily—married, he'd become the king's ally in the quest to seek a suitable wife for his brothers. Although Rafiq suspected that Shafir was only trying to drive home how fortunate he'd been to find his Megan. If he could find a woman as unique, as in tune with him as Megan was with Shafir, he'd get married in a shot....

Khalid bestowed a killing look on Shafir, who laughed and helped himself to a cup of the rich, fragrant coffee that the bank's newest secretary was busy pouring into small brass cups.

"Thank you, Miss Turner." To his father Khalid added, "I don't need a list. I will find my own wife."

Rafiq craned his neck, peering at the list. "Who else is on there?"

"Farrah? She's far too young—I don't want a child bride."

"Leila Mummhar."

Rafiq's suggestion had captured his father's attention.

"Pah." The King flung out his arms. "Don't *you* give him advice. I was certain you'd be married long before Shafir. Now look at you—no woman at your side since your beloved departed."

"Shenilla and I had...differences." It was the best way to describe the pushy interest that Shenilla's father had started to exert as soon as they'd considered him hooked. Shenilla was a qualified accountant, she was beautiful, her family was well respected in Dhahara. On paper it was the perfect match.

Yet he'd run....

"Differences?" His father growled. "What is a little difference? Your beloved mother and I had many differences while we were courting. We overcame them and—"

"But your marriage was expected," Rafiq interrupted. "It was arranged between your families from the time you were very young. You could not end such a relationship."

The king shook his head. "It made marriage no easier. But we worked at it. Happiness is something to strive for, my son, every day of your life. And you were so in love. Ay me, I was so certain that this time it would be right."

How could Rafiq confess that he'd been sure that Shenilla had been perfect for him, yet once their families had become involved as quickly as he'd fallen in love with her, he'd fallen out again? And it hadn't been the first time. Before that there had been Rosa and before her, Neela. He wasn't indiscriminate. His cautious courtships lasted for lengthy periods—that was expected after the care he put into the choice. But just when they got to the point where formalities like engagements became expected, when the pressure to set a wedding date was applied, the love dwindled, leaving only a restless need to escape the cloying trap the relationship had become.

"Khalid, you may object now but you know your duty." The king patted his firstborn son on the shoulder. "Choose any one of those women and you will be richly rewarded."

Rafiq eyed the list and thought of the requirements he'd set for women he considered in the past—after all he was a practical man, his wife would have to fit into his world. Wealthy. Beautiful. Well connected. "Yasmin comes from a powerful family."

Khalid shook his head fiercely. "No, it's not her family I'd be marrying. And I want more than power, wealth and looks in a bride. She must be able to keep me interested for many years, long after worldly goods are forgotten."

Interested? Rafiq's thoughts veered to the last woman who had occupied his bed.

Tiffany had kept him interested from the moment he'd met her. Yes, he'd told her she was beautiful. And he'd meant it. But she was nothing like the other beauties he'd dated. Her features reflected her every emotion, and the graceful way she moved had held him entranced. She certainly fulfilled none of the other criteria he looked for in a wife…she'd never be suitable.

It shamed him that in one short night with little effort she'd stripped him of the restraint and control he prided himself on. It had disturbed him deeply that a woman whom he didn't love, held no fondness for, a woman he suspected of being a con artist, a blackmailer, could hold such power over him.

She'd insisted she'd had no intention of bedding him; she'd been as deliciously tight as a virgin, yet she'd produced a condom at the critical moment. And she'd lied about deleting the photos she'd taken of him and Sir Julian. The more he thought about it, the more he decided he'd been played for a fool by an expert.

He'd given her his business card.

Fool!

He stared blindly at the list he held until Shafir stretched across the boardroom table and snagged it. His brother studied it…and hooted with laughter, pulling Rafiq out the trance that held him immobile. "I can't believe Leila is on here—she's more work than all the bandits that hide on the border of Marulla."

"It would make political sense—we would be able to watch her relations," the king growled.

"Father, we don't want the trouble that her uncles would bring." Rafiq shook his head as he referred to the spats that the two sheikhs were infamous for waging. "Pick someone with less baggage."

Khalid fixed his attention on Shafir. "Maybe I should do what you did…choose a woman with family on the other side of the world. That way I will have no problem with my inlaws."

Suppressing the urge to grin, Rafiq waited for his father to launch into a tirade about the sanctity of family. But his father wore an arrested expression. "Rafiq, did you not say that Sir Julian Carling has a daughter?"

"Yes." Rafiq thought of the woman he'd once met. "Elizabeth Carling."

Despite the dislike he'd taken to Sir Julian, there'd been nothing wrong with the daughter. Elizabeth had everything he usually looked for. Wealth, beauty, connections. Yet there'd been no spark. Not like what he'd experienced with Tiffany—if such a wild madness could be termed a spark. It had been more like a conflagration.

At last he nodded. "Yes, she would be a good choice for Khalid."

"Add her to the list," his father commanded Shafir. "Rafiq says her father is coming to Dhahara to inspect the site for the new Carling Hotel. Her father is a very wealthy man." King Selim gave his eldest son an arch look, and leaned back in his chair. "I will invite Lady Carling and his daughter, too."

Even as Khalid glared at him, the young secretary reappeared in the doorway, concern in her eyes. "The CEO of Pyramid Oil is here for his appointment. What shall I tell him?"

"That's right, run, before I kill you for adding to the pressure," his brother muttered, but Rafiq only laughed.

"Discussing your future took the heat off me, so thanks."

Khalid snorted in disgust.

Still grinning, Rafiq turned to the young secretary. "Miss Turner, give us five more minutes—by then I will be done."

Tiffany stepped out of the cab into the dry, arid midday heat of Dhahara. Hot wind redolent of spices and a tang of the desert swept around her. In front of her towered the Royal Bank of Dhahara. The butterflies that had been floating around in her stomach started to whip their wings in earnest.

Sure, she'd known from his gold-embossed card that

Rafiq would be an important man. President, Royal Bank of Dhahara. But not *this* important.

Yet coming here had been the right thing to do. She'd never doubted her path from the moment the doctor had confirmed her deepest fear. But being confronted with the material reality of where Rafiq worked, knowing that it would be only minutes before she saw him again, made her palms grow moist and her heart thump loudly in her chest.

She paid the driver and couldn't help being relieved that she'd had the foresight to check into a city hotel and stow her luggage in her room before coming here. Pulling a filmy scarf over her hair, she passed the bank's uniformed guard and headed for the glass sliding doors.

Inside, behind the sleek, circular black marble reception counter, stood a young, clean-shaven man in a dark suit and white headgear. Tiffany approached him, determined to brazen this out. "I have an appointment."

His brow creased as he scanned the computer screen in front of him, searching for an appointment she knew would not be listed for today…or any day. Finally he shook his head.

But Tiffany had not come this far to be deterred. She held her ground, refusing to turn away.

"Call Rafiq Al Dhahara." Her conjuring up the name she'd memorized from the business card caused him to do a double take. "Tell him Tiffany Smith is here to see him." She mustered up every bit of authority that she had. "He won't be pleased if he learns you sent me away without bothering to check."

That was stretching the truth, because Rafiq might well refuse to see her. Even if he did agree to speak to her, he would certainly not be pleased to find her here in Dhahara.

But the bank official wasn't to know that.

Tiffany waited, arms folded across a stomach that was still behaving in the most peculiar fashion, as it fluttered and tumbled over.

He picked up a telephone and spoke in Arabic. When he'd finished, his expression had changed. "The sheikh will see you."

The sheikh?

Oh, my. This time her stomach turned a full somersault. "Sheikh?" she spluttered. "I thought he was—" she searched a mind gone suddenly blank for the impressive title on his business card "—the president of the Royal Bank of Dhahara."

The bank official gave her a peculiar look. "The royal family owns the bank."

"What does that have to do with Rafiq?"

He blinked at her casual use of his name, and then replied, "The sheikh is part of the royal family."

Before she could faintly repeat "royal family," the elevator doors to the left of the marble reception counter slid open, and Rafiq himself stepped out.

His face was haughtier than she remembered, his eyes darker, his cheekbones more aristocratic. Sheikh? Royal family? He certainly looked every inch the part in a dark suit with a conservative white shirt that even in this sweltering heat appeared crisp and fresh. Yet his head was uncovered, and his hair gleamed like a black hawk's wing. After all the soul-searching it had taken to bring her here, now that she faced him she couldn't think of a word to say.

So she settled for the most inane.

"Hi."

"Tiffany."

The sphinxlike gaze revealed no surprise. He'd told

her he never wanted to see her again. *Ever.* Now she stood before him, shifting from one foot to the other. The displeasure she'd expected was absent. Typically, he showed no emotion at all. The wall of stony reserve was as high as ever.

He bowed his head. "Please, come with me."

If it hadn't been for one never-to-be-forgotten night in Hong Kong, she'd never have known that his reserve could be breached.

That night…

The memory of the catastrophic extremes, heaven and hell, pleasure and shame, still had the power to make her shudder.

Tiffany had been sure nothing would make her contact him again. Nothing. But she'd been so wrong. She pressed her hand to her belly.

Her baby…

He ushered her into the elevator. Unexpectedly, the elevator dropped instead of rising. Her stomach rolled wildly. Tiffany gritted her teeth. Seconds later the doors opened to reveal a well-lit parking level where a black Mercedes-Benz idled, waiting. Rafiq strode forward and opened the rear door.

She hesitated. "Where—?"

His dark gaze was hooded. "There is no privacy here."

He was ashamed of her.

Despite a tinge of apprehension Tiffany swallowed her protests and, straightening her spine, stepped past him and slid into the leather backseat.

She'd come to Dhahara because of her baby. Not for herself. Not for Rafiq. For their unborn child.

She couldn't afford to let fear dominate her.

For her daughter she had put aside her desire never

to encounter Rafiq again. For the baby's sake, she would keep her relationship with Rafiq cordial. Unemotional. Her daughter deserved the right to know her father. Nor could she allow herself to indulge in wild notions that he might kidnap her child, hide her away.

He was a businessman. He'd told her he'd been educated in England and the United States. He headed a large bank. Even it if was a position he'd gotten through nepotism, neither he—nor his royal family—could afford the kind of international outcry that would come from taking her baby from her. He was a single man—or at least she hoped he was—what would he do with a baby?

The silence was oppressive. Fifteen minutes later the Mercedes came to a smooth stop, and the rear doors opened. Rafiq's hand closed around her elbow—to escort her or ensure she didn't escape? Tiffany wasn't sure. As he hurried her up a flight of stairs, she caught a glimpse of two guards in red berets standing in front of stone pillars that flanked a vast wooden front door. Then the door swung inward and they were inside a vaulted entrance hall.

She gazed around, wide-eyed. Despite the mansions she'd seen, this dwelling took luxury to new heights. "Where are we?"

"This is my home."

A hasty glance revealed magnificent dark wooden floors covered in Persian rugs, original art hanging on deep blue walls. Refusing to be impressed, Tiffany focused her attention on Rafiq. "Is there somewhere we can talk?"

His lips quirked, and something devilish gleamed in his eyes. "Talk? Our best communication is done in other ways. I thought that must be why you are here."

Damn him for the reminder.

Tiffany compressed her lips. "I need to talk to you."

"Whenever we talk, it seems to cost me money." The humor had vanished, and he gave her a brooding look.

His words only underscored what she already knew: he thought her the worst kind of woman. What would he say when he discovered she was pregnant with his child? A frisson of alarm chilled her.

"I haven't come all this way for money, Rafiq."

"I'm very relieved to hear that."

He strode down a hall hung with richly woven tapestries that held the patina of age. Tiffany resisted the urge to slow and inspect them.

"But for the moment I will reserve judgment," he was saying. "I will be more convinced of that once I have heard what you have to say to me."

He didn't believe her. He thought this was about money.

"Hey, I sent you a check for what you gave me," she protested. She hadn't wanted to be in his debt.

"Sure you did."

"I sent it last week. Maybe it's still in the mail." She'd meant to send it earlier. Discovering she was pregnant had wiped all other thoughts out of her head. But now she was seriously starting to wish that she had called...not come all this way to give him the news about his impending fatherhood.

Yet it had seemed the right thing to do. She'd wanted to break the news in person, not over the phone separated by thousands of miles, unable to register the nuances of his expression. And certainly not by an e-mail that might go astray.

This was too important. Her child's whole life, her baby's relationship with her father, would be determined by the course of this conversation.

And she wasn't about to let Rafiq Al Dhahara cause

her to regret the decision she'd made to come here to tell him.

Pushing open a door, he gestured for her to precede him. Tiffany entered a book-lined room that was clearly a man's domain. *His* domain. Before her nerve could give out, she drew a deep breath and spun to face him.

"I'm pregnant," she announced.

Rafiq went very still, and his eyes narrowed to dark cracks that revealed nothing.

All at once the dangerous man she'd seen glimpses of in Hong Kong, the man she'd known lurked under the polite, charming veneer, surfaced.

"We used a condom," he said, softly.

She spread her hands helplessly. "It must've been faulty."

"Did you know it was faulty?"

"What's that supposed to mean?"

"Did you tamper with it?"

"How?" Outrage filled the question. "It was sealed!"

"Nothing a pinprick couldn't have taken care of."

"You're sick."

His mouth tightened. "Be careful how you talk to me."

Tiffany's front teeth worried at her bottom lip. His gaze flickered to her mouth, before returning to clash with hers. "How much do you want?"

"What?"

She stared at him, not sure she'd heard right. His eyes were fixed on her, his mouth tight. No sign of softness in the features that were so difficult to read. He'd pay money so that he'd never have to see his child again?

What kind of man did that?

Tiffany turned away, defeated. At least she would always carry the knowledge in her heart that she'd tried. And if her daughter one day wanted to know who her father was, she'd tell her. Rafiq might be a sheikh. He might be desert royalty. But he would be the loser...he'd have forfeited the chance to know his child.

But he'd been given the choice.

"I've been a fool."

Tiffany spun back and focused on him. He'd positioned himself behind an antique desk. One hand was raking through his hair. Straight and dark, it shone like silk under the overhead lights.

Unable to bear to look at him, she closed her eyes.

He'd been a fool? What did that make her?

"And I have absolutely no excuse. I even know how the scam works. Start with small amounts, get the idiot hooked and then, when he can't back out, increase the amount."

Her mouth fell open as she absorbed what he was saying. "You honestly think I'd travel *here* to blackmail you?" Her hand closed protectively over her belly. "That I'd blackmail the father of my child?"

From beyond the barrier of the desk, his glance fell to her still-flat stomach, and then lifted to meet her eyes. Black. Implacable. Furious. Tiffany felt the searing heat of his contempt. "Enough. Don't expect me to believe there is a child."

Rafiq thought—

She shook her head to clear it. "You really do think I came all this way to blackmail you."

He arched a brow. "Didn't you?"

"No!"

"Previous experience makes that impossible for me to believe."

What was the point of arguing that she hadn't wanted to blackmail him in the past, either? Tiffany placed her fingertips to her pounding temples. God, why had she allowed her conviction that she was doing the right thing to persuade her to come? He didn't care about the child. All he cared about was protecting himself.

There was nothing here for her daughter…nothing worth fighting for.

She started to back away.

"Where are you going?"

"To my hotel. I'm pregnant. It was a long flight. I'm tired. My feet ache. I need a shower and a sleep." She listed the reasons in a flat, dead tone.

He was around the desk before she could move and caught up to her with two long strides. Planting himself in front of her, he folded his arms across his chest. "You will stay here."

Tiffany shook her head. "I can't stay here." He was a man—an unmarried man. It would not be sanctioned. "Besides, my luggage is already at the hotel."

His jaw had set. "I am not letting you stay in the city alone. I want you where I can watch you. Give me the name of the hotel and I will have your luggage sent here."

"I'd be your prisoner."

"Not a prisoner," he corrected, "my guest."

"It's hardly appropriate for me to stay here, even I know—"

Holding up a hand, he stopped her mid-sentence. "My aunt Lily will come stay. The widow of my father's brother, and the perfect chaperone. Zara, her daughter, is away studying at present, and Aunt Lily is missing her. She's Australian, so you should get along well. But don't think you can wind her around your little finger. I will be there all the time you are together. Rest tonight, and I will escort you back to the airport myself tomorrow."

Taking in his hard face, Tiffany made herself straighten. She'd come all this way, and he didn't even believe she was pregnant. Right now she was too weary to argue further but she'd be damned if she'd let him see that. He'd only interpret it as weakness. Tomorrow she'd be ready to fight again.

At least she'd have a chance to meet a part of his family, his aunt. For her daughter's future relationship with her father, Tiffany knew she would do her best to get along with the woman.

Before he took her by the scruff of her neck and threw her out of his country.

Five

Tiffany hadn't been lying about being weary, Rafiq saw that evening. Seated across from him at the dinner table, alongside his aunt Lily, who was clearly bursting with curiosity about her presence in his home, Tiffany barely picked at her food.

There were shadows beneath her eyes. Pale purple hollows that gave her a heart-wrenching fragility that tugged at him—even though he refused to put a name to the emotion.

The array of dishes at her elbow remained untouched. The succulent pieces of skewered lamb. The breads baked with great care in his kitchens. The char-roasted vegetables on earthenware platters. Even her wineglass remained full. Something of the fine spread should have tempted her. But nothing had.

Finally, his aunt could clearly contain herself no longer. "My daughter is at university in Los Angeles. Did you meet Rafiq when he studied abroad?"

Rafiq answered before she could reply. "Tiffany and I are…business acquaintances. She's been traveling—and decided to visit." It didn't satisfy his aunt's curiosity but she wouldn't ask again.

"You look tired, dear."

"I am." Tiffany gave Lily a smile. "I can't wait to go to bed."

"After dinner I'll show you where the women's quarters are."

"Thank you."

The subdued note in her voice made Rafiq want to confront the turmoil that had been whirling around inside his head. He'd been rough on her earlier. Even his aunt could see that her travels had worn her out.

A trickle of shame seeped through Rafiq, then he forced it ruthlessly aside. What else was he supposed to have done? Accepted the lie that she was pregnant? Paid through the nose for the privilege of silencing her new blackmail attempt?

Never.

He'd taken the only course of action open to him: he'd brought her here, away from the bank, away from any possible contact with his father, brothers and staff to learn what she wanted.

Pregnant? Hah! He would not let her get away with such a ruse. Now she was confined to his home. And he would make sure she wasn't left alone with his aunt. He made a mental note to assign one of the maids to keep the women company. His aunt would never gossip in front of the servants.

Tomorrow she would leave. He'd escort her to the airport himself. He certainly wouldn't allow himself any regrets. Tiffany was not the stranded innocent she'd once almost managed to con him into believing she was. He'd already allowed her to squeeze him for money once.

By foolishly possessing her, taking her under a starlit sky, he'd made a fatal mistake. One that she would milk for the rest of her life—if he let her.

Rafiq had no intention of becoming trapped in the prison she'd created with her soft touches and sweet, drugging kisses.

He became aware that Tiffany was talking to his aunt. He tensed, and started to pay attention.

"You must miss your daughter," Tiffany was saying.

Lily nodded. "But I'll be joining her when the holidays come. She wanted a little time to find her feet."

"How lucky for her that you respect her need for independence."

"I still worry about her. She had a bad romantic experience a while back."

That was enough! He wasn't having this woman interrogating his family, discovering pains better left hidden.

"Wine?" Rafiq brusquely offered Tiffany.

She shook her head, "No, thanks." And focused on his aunt. "Do you have any other children?"

"No, only Zara."

"I'm an only child, too."

"Oh, what a pity Zara wasn't here for you to meet. You would've gotten along like a house on fire."

Rafiq narrowed his gaze. If Tiffany even thought she might threaten his family's well-being she would learn how very ruthless he could be.

"I would've liked that."

She sounded so sincere. His aunt was glowing with delight. Lily put a hand on his arm, "I'm sure your father and brothers would like to meet Tiffany."

"I'd like that but—"

His killing glare interrupted the woman who had caused all this trouble. "Tiffany will not be staying for very long," he said with a snap of his teeth.

Aunt Lily looked crestfallen. "What a pity."

Rafiq wished savagely that he'd been less respectful of Tiffany's modesty. He should've known better than to introduce her to any member of his family.

"She'll be leaving us tomorrow."

The bedchamber Lily and the little plump maid called Mina showed Tiffany into was rich and luxurious. Filmy gold drapes surrounded a high bed covered by white linen while beautiful handwoven rugs covered the intricately patterned wooden floors. On the opposite walls, shutters were flung back to reveal a view of a courtyard containing a pool surrounded by padded loungers. Water trickled over a tiered fountain on the far side of the pool, the soothing sound adding to the welcome.

It felt as if she'd been transported into another, far more exotic, world.

Alone, Tiffany stripped off her crumpled clothes and pulled on a nightie. She felt dazed and disoriented and just a little bit queasy. Jet lag was setting in with vengeance.

Through an open door, she caught a glimpse of an immense tub with leaping dolphins—dolphins!—for faucets before weariness sank like a cloud around her. She padded through to the large bathroom to brush her teeth before heading for the bedchamber and clambering between the soft sheets where sleep claimed her.

The next thing she knew she was being wakened by the loud sound of knocking. Seconds later the door crashed open.

Tiffany sat up, dragging the covers up to her chin, thoroughly startled at being yanked from deep sleep.

"What do you want?" she demanded of the man looming in the doorway.

"Neither of the maids could awaken you." Whatever had glittered in Rafiq's eyes when the door first opened had already subsided.

"I was tired," she said defensively. "I told you that last night."

"It's late." He glanced at his watch. "Eleven o'clock. I thought you might've run out—" He broke off.

Eleven o'clock was all she heard. "It can't be that late."

He strode closer, brandishing the square face of his Cartier timepiece in her direction. "Look."

The wrist beneath the leather strap was tanned, a mix of sinew and muscle. Oh, God, surely she wasn't being drawn back under his thrall?

"I believe you," she said hastily, her grip tightening on the bedcovers as she pulled them up to her chin so that no bare flesh was visible. Her stomach had started its now-familiar morning lurching routine.

"Will you please *go?*"

And then it was too late. Tiffany bolted from the bed and into the adjoining bathroom, where she was miserably and ignominiously sick.

When she finally raised her head, it was—horror of horrors—to find Rafiq beside her, holding out a white facecloth. She took it and wiped it over her face, appreciating the cool wetness.

"Thanks," she mumbled.

"You look terrible."

This time her "Thanks" held no gratitude.

"I don't like this. I'm going to call a doctor." He was already moving away with that sleek, predatory stride.

"Don't," Tiffany said.

He halted just short of the bathroom door.

"There's nothing wrong with me." She gave him a grim smile.

"Maybe it was something you ate." Two long paces had him at her side. "You may need an antibiotic."

"No antibiotic!" Nothing was going to harm her baby. "I promise you this is a perfectly normal part of being pregnant."

His hands closed around her shoulders. "Oh, don't try that tall tale again."

"It's the truth. I can't help that you're too dumb to see what's right in front of your nose." She poked a finger at his chest, but to her dismay he did not back away. Instead she became conscious of his muscled body beneath the crisply ironed business shirt. A body she'd touched all over the night they had been together...

She withdrew her finger as though it had been burned.

"I'm not dumb," he growled.

Right. "And I'm not pregnant," she countered.

"I *knew* you were faking it."

The triumph in his voice made her see red. "Oh, for heaven's sake!"

Tiffany broke out of his grasp and, slipping past him, headed for the bedroom. Grabbing her purse off the dressing table she upended it onto the bed and scrabbled through the displaced contents. Snatching up a black-and-white image in a small frame she spun around to wave it in front of his nose.

"Look at this."

"What is it?"

Couldn't he see? He had to be blind...as well as obtuse.

"A photo of your daughter."

"A photo of my daughter?" For once that air of composure had deserted him. "I don't have a daughter."

She pushed the picture into his hands. "It's an image from a scan. A scan of my baby—" *their baby* "—taken last week. See? There's her head, her hipbone, her arms. That's your daughter you're holding."

His expression changed. When he finally raised his head, his eyes were glazed with shock.

"You really *are* pregnant."

Six

"No, I'm only faking it. Remember?"

Rafiq glared at Tiffany, unamused by the flippant retort—and the sharp edge he detected beneath it. He tightened his grip on the photo, conscious of a sense that his world was shifting.

"So how do you know it's a girl? Can they tell?"

She stared down her nose at him in a way that made him want to kiss her, or throttle her. Then she said, "My intuition tells me she is."

Her intuition? The ridiculous reply brought him back to reality, and he shut down the string of questions that he'd been about to ask. Rafiq almost snorted in disgust at how readily he'd crumbled. She was softening him up—and worse, it was working.

"You don't think I'm going to fall for this?" He shoved the picture back at her. "This could be any man's baby."

Her fingers closed around the small framed image with

great care. She slid it into the bag and walked back to the dressing table where she set the bag down. Her back to him, she said, "Doctors will be able to estimate the time of conception close enough to that night—"

"They won't be able to pinpoint exactly. The baby could've been conceived anytime around then." He paused as she wheeled around to face him. "It doesn't mean it is *my* child." He sneered. "I hardly met you under the most pristine conditions."

The gold flecks in those velvet eyes grew dull. "I told you that it was my first night at Le Club."

"I don't know you at all." He shrugged. "Even if it was the truth, who knows what's behind it?"

Tiffany flushed, and the gold in her tawny eyes had brightened to an accusatory flame. She looked spirited, alive, and Rafiq fisted his hands at his sides to stop himself from reaching for her. Instead he said, "I want to have DNA tests done before I pay a dollar."

"Have I demanded even one dollar from you since I got here?" she asked, her eyes blazing with what he realized in surprise was rage. Glorious, incandescent rage that had him blinking in admiration.

"I'm sure you intend to demand far more than that."

"There's no trust in you, is there?"

"Not a great deal," he said honestly. "When you grow up as wealthy as I have there's always someone with a new angle. A new scam."

"Everyone wants something from you?"

He shrugged. "I'm used to it."

There was a perturbing perception in her gaze. As if she understood exactly how he felt. And sympathized. But she couldn't. He'd found her in the backstreets of Hong Kong—hardly the place for someone who could have any insight into his world.

Crossing to the bedroom door that he'd left wide open, he paused. "I'll arrange for the DNA tests to be done as soon as possible." That would give him the answer he wanted and put an end to this farce.

"But you were going to take me to the airport."

Rafiq's gaze narrowed. Tiffany looked surprisingly agitated. "You're not staying in Dhahara long. You'll be on the first plane out once I have confirmation that your child is not mine. You're not going to hold that threat over my head for the rest of my life."

Once a week Rafiq met his brother Khalid for breakfast in one of Dhahara's seven star hotels. As the two men were heavily invested in the political and economic well-being of the desert kingdom, talk was usually lively. But Rafiq was too abstracted by the rapidly approaching appointment for his and Tiffany's DNA tests that he'd arranged after their argument yesterday.

Before he could temper it, he found himself asking, "Khalid, have you ever thought what might happen if you get a woman who is not on father's list pregnant?"

His brother's mouth fell open in surprise. He looked around and lowered his voice. "I take great care not to get a woman pregnant."

So did Rafiq. It hadn't helped. He'd been a fool. "But what if you did," he pressed, pushing his empty plate away. "What would you do?"

Khalid looked disconcerted. "I don't know. One thing is for sure, an abortion would be out of the question. I suppose it would depend on the situation. The woman in question would have to be suitable for me to consider marrying her."

Suitable. Just thinking of the night he'd met Tiffany

made Rafiq squirm. She couldn't have been more totally *un*suitable if he'd scoured the entire earth. "That is true."

And there lay his problem.

"Of course," continued his brother, then pausing as a white-garbed waiter filled their cups with black, fragrant coffee and waiting until he'd left, "there has never been an illegitimate heir in our family. That's something else to consider. I suppose even an unsuitable marriage would be better than that," mused Khalid. "Later I could always find a second, more suitable wife who would perform the state duties."

Rafiq had never considered marriage to Tiffany an option. As he sipped his coffee, another thought occurred to him. "If there's a marriage, then there's divorce, too."

Khalid frowned. "As a last resort. It's never popular for a ruler to divorce a consort."

But, even though his brother didn't know it, they weren't talking about Khalid. They were talking about *his* situation. And Rafiq was not heir to the throne. It wouldn't attract the same degree of censure.

Marriage to legitimize the child followed by divorce might work…*if* the child turned out to be his.

Rafiq set his cup down and flicked back a starched cuff to glance at his Cartier watch. Time to go. Tiffany would be waiting for him to collect her from his residence. "It's later than I thought. I have an appointment—I must go."

"If I divorced her, I'd make sure the child—if it was a boy—was well out of her control," said Khalid thoughtfully.

Arrested, Rafiq turned to gaze at his brother. *Of course.* "Thank you."

While Khalid shook his head in bemusement, Rafiq strode across the dining hall with a light heart. Sometimes the solution to a seemingly insurmountable problem was far simpler than a man dreamed.

The doctor's rooms were surprisingly modern. A glass desk paired with crisp-white walls hung with framed sketches of flowers gave the room a contemporary feel. Nothing like the heavy dark furniture Tiffany had expected. Even more astonishing was the fact that the doctor was female. Although on second thought, that shouldn't have surprised her. No doubt many Dhaharan men preferred their wives to be examined by a woman doctor.

Yet it was the doctor's words that had caused the tension that presently gripped Tiffany. Shaking her head until her hair whipped about her face, she turned to Rafiq and said defiantly, "I'm not agreeing to that."

Rafiq gave Dr. Farouk a charming smile. "Excuse us for a moment, please."

The doctor rose to her feet. "Of course, Your Highness. I'll be next door when you need me."

A few words and a smile from him, and the doctor simply obeyed? Vacating her own office? Tiffany was taken aback at the display of his power.

No wonder Rafiq believed he could get whatever he wanted.

"I'm not signing the consent for surgery." Tiffany gestured to the paper that lay on the desk.

Rafiq raked a hand through his hair, rumpling the sleek perfection. "I was prepared to undergo the indignity of a test—why can't you be more cooperative?"

"A swab taken from your inner cheek?" She snorted. "That's nothing. If it was just a simple DNA test, I wouldn't have a problem. But you heard the doctor. Getting the baby's DNA is not going to be that easy."

The doctor had laid the options out for them. Getting the baby's DNA would require a surgical procedure. Because Tiffany was only ten weeks pregnant, amniocentesis could not be performed. Instead, a thin needle, guided by ultrasound, would pass through her cervix to retrieve little fingers of tissue from the wall of the uterus beyond. Like her baby, the tissue, which the doctor had called chorionic villi, originated from the egg that Rafiq's sperm had fertilized.

"You're not going to change my mind," she warned him.

"Be reasonable—"

"Reasonable? You heard the doctor. The procedure holds risks to my baby."

He waved a hand. "Very slim percentages."

"Miscarriage is not a percentage I'm prepared to risk."

Rafiq's eyebrows lowered to form a thick line over his eyes, making him look fierce and formidable. "How else am I supposed to find out whether the baby is mine?"

She glared at him, determined not to let him know that her heart was knocking against her ribs. "You're prepared to risk this life growing within me, so that you can evade the responsibility of fatherhood?"

"That's not true—"

"Of course it's true." She averted her gaze. "You could easily wait until the baby is born, *then* have the necessary tests done. But no, that doesn't suit the great sheikh. So you want to risk my baby's life to get the answer you're expecting. Well, I'm not going to let that happen!"

"You're hardly in a position to dictate terms," he breathed from barely an inch away.

"I'm in the best position," she fired back. "I'm not signing that consent form."

"Then you'll lose any chance of a quick cash settlement."

"I don't need your monetary support. I just wanted you to know…" Her voice trailed away.

How to explain? Her childhood had been less than perfect, disrupted by her father's affairs. Rafiq might've been distant, but he'd struck her as honorable. She'd wanted her daughter to have a father. Resting her fingertips on her stomach, Tiffany said softly, "One day this baby will want to know who her father is—and I would never keep that from her."

"Nor would I. This is not an attempt to evade responsibility."

It appeared her accusation had irked him.

He leaned toward her. "Tiffany, understand this, as long as a child is mine, I will take care of it."

"It?" His use of the derogatory term revealed the disparity between them. "No baby of mine could ever be an 'it.' She's a person. Infinitely precious."

"That's why you have no choice but to take this test. So that I can give the child the best if it is mine." But he was looking less certain than he had only minutes ago.

"You could take my word," she snapped, but already Rafiq was shaking his head, his eyes beginning to glitter with what she recognized as annoyance. She held her ground. This was not an issue she was prepared to negotiate. "Then you have no choice but to wait until the baby is born."

Rafiq got to his feet and started to pace. "Neither of those are options I'm prepared to accept. I want hard evidence that your child is not mine—so I can escort you out of the country."

"I'm not risking a miscarriage. You can't force me to

undergo this procedure," she stated, and hoped like hell she was right. Nor could he make her stay.

Or could he? This was his domain, after all. When she'd come to Dhahara she hadn't known the extent of his power…that he was the king's son, a royal sheikh. And when she'd discovered that, she'd convinced herself that he wouldn't be interested in bringing up the child.

But now she was starting to get cold feet. His family made the laws in this country. Rafiq could do what he wanted to her—with her—and get away with it. Could he force her to have surgery against her will? Would he keep her in Dhahara if she wanted to leave?

Before her first flutterings of fear could develop into full-fledged panic, Rafiq had turned to face her. He stood still and erect.

Tiffany took in the magnificence of the man. The harsh hawk-like features. His dark suit that had to be handmade. The shine of his shoes. He could've stepped out of a magazine spread. Yet she didn't like what he was trying to persuade her to do.

"Look," she said, tempering her voice, "I told you my passport was stolen—you didn't believe me. Yet it was true."

"You blackmailed me."

"That's the interpretation you put on it." She pushed the fringe of her bangs out her eyes. "I bet you never thought you'd see the cash again. But I've paid you back in full. Now I'm pregnant—and you think that's a scam, too. Yet here we are in the doctor's office and it's true."

"How convenient."

She ignored his sarcasm and continued, "As much as you tell yourself I slept with the whole of Hong Kong, you must know that it's possible that you're the father of my child—"

Nothing she said appeared to be denting that shell. His eyes were still hard with suspicion. "We used a condom."

"And, of course, you'd like to put your faith in the percentages that say overwhelmingly that they're fail-safe?" She shook her head. "Because it suits you. Well, not this time. Something went wrong. Just like something could go wrong when the doctor takes the chorionic villi sample."

A frisson of unease slithered through her. She moved from one foot to the other under his stare. The fact that he was selfish enough to be prepared to jeopardize their daughter, a living being, had made her realize that maybe he wasn't the kind of father she wanted for her baby. How could she even contemplate occasionally leaving her daughter in his solo care?

The sooner she—and her unborn baby—left this country, the better for them both.

He didn't believe the baby was his, so he had no reason to stop her. The decision made, the tension that had been building within her started to ease.

"I'll leave Dhahara now. Today, on the first flight I can get. Once the baby is born, taking a sample from inside her cheek will be a breeze, compared to this invasive procedure. The solution is simple. Let's defer this discussion until then."

But instead of looking happy at the thought, he frowned. "Where would you go?"

His concern must stem for the prospect of the scandal he would face once it became known he'd fathered her unborn child. She knew all about gossip and scandal—it had been part of her world for too long. The best way to deal with it was to lie low.

"I can go to my parents' home in New Zealand." She

hesitated, contemplating telling him more about her parents, then decided it wasn't relevant, not now. She didn't even know where her father was. Thinking about her parents made her realize that soon there would be no home in Auckland. Her mother needed the money that the sale of the house would bring. "Although my mother will probably need to sell up the house in Auckland."

"Tiffany—"

She didn't need his pity. She rushed on. "There's a quiet seaside village I used to visit as a child." Her vision blurred at the memory of those carefree days. Everything had been so simple then. So happy. That was what she wanted for her child. "I'll go there."

He didn't look any happier. "I thought you wanted to meet my family. At least, that's what you had my aunt believing."

"I did. I mean, I do," Tiffany hastily amended her reply. "They're my daughter's family, too. But you've made it clear you can't wait to get rid of me. Why the sudden about-face?"

Tension quivered through him. "So why leave now? After coming all this way? What if it *is* my baby?"

Her daughter didn't deserve a father who would risk her very existence to evade paternity. No father would be better than that. She'd make up for her baby's lack of a father. She'd do everything in her power to be the best parent her daughter could have.

Rafiq was waiting for her response. She shrugged. "Do you care?"

Anger ignited in the back of his dark eyes, giving them a feral depth. "Yes. I care."

Sensing she'd miscalculated, she said quickly, "Well, after the baby is born, and once the tests have been done and your paternity confirmed, then you can decide whether you want a part in her life."

"You can bet your life on it I will."

Her instinct to flee wavered. Just as she'd decided he didn't want this baby, he ruined it by getting all passionate and showing her a glimpse of caring.

"My child will not be born illegitimate," he whispered. "There's never been an illegitimate heir born in my family." His carved features revealed no emotion. "That's why I need to know if the child is mine."

The unease deepened to panic. He didn't care about the baby at all. Only about legalities.

"It doesn't matter that the baby will be illegitimate. *She* will be loved." Tiffany gave *she* a not-so-subtle emphasis. "I'd never subject her to a marriage between parents who care nothing for each other." Her own parents had been wildly in love when they'd gotten married. Yet their marriage had become a battleground. Her father had been unable to resist other women, had helped himself to them like a child to candy.

When she married she would choose carefully. A nice, ordinary family man.

"It matters." His fist closed around her wrist.

Tiffany shuddered under the pressure of his fingers. "Well, this appointment is over. I'm not having this test done now, so this whole discussion is irrelevant until the baby is born."

In the meantime she was going to get her baby out of this country, out from under his control. She pulled her hand free of his and rose to her feet.

"Then I'm going to have to take your word that it's my baby." His features were stern as gazed up at her from where he sat, master of all he surveyed, in the doctor's office. "If you are lying to me, you will regret it."

"I'm not lying—"

He cut across her heated denial. "There's no option but for us to get married in the meantime."

"Get married?"

Tiffany was staring at him as if he'd taken leave of his senses.

Perhaps he had. Rafiq suppressed the urge to smile grimly at her wide-eyed shock. Did she not grasp the honor he'd offered her? But what choice did he have? He would use every advantage offered by his country's laws if the baby proved to be his own—he would marry her, divorce her and keep the baby as his own.

"I'm not marrying *you*."

She made it sound as if he were a particularly offensive variety of the male sex. As she pushed past him, he snagged her fingers between his, and growled, "Think of it as your lucky day. Lots of women want to marry me."

Tiffany opened her mouth, shut it and made a peculiar sound.

Rafiq leaned closer until her tantalizing fragrance enveloped him. "You wouldn't be thinking of claiming that you're so different from all those women, would you, Tiffany?"

The brief flash of awareness in her eyes turned quickly to something darker. He could see she remembered quite clearly what had happened the last time she'd vowed she was so different from the women who considered him charming. In fact, his determination to prove conclusively that she *did* find him charming was what had led to this present blackmail attempt of hers.

That realization alone should've leashed the reckless impulse to provoke her. But it didn't. Instead he remembered what she'd tasted like…the softness of her skin beneath his fingers…and every detail of what had followed on that hot, balmy night.

She was irresistible.

With a silent curse he realized he wanted to kiss her again. "Tiffany…"

He got to his feet and placed his hands on her shoulders, felt the shudder that quaked through her.

She didn't pull away. So he drew her closer. Breathed in the soft seductive scent of her. Filled his senses with her sweetness until he could wait no more.

Kissing Tiffany was like rediscovering a secret, shaded oasis filled with fragrant gardenias and leafy green trees. He hadn't even known that he'd missed her as intensely. Yet now he found himself drowning in her.

His eyes closed, he took his time to rediscover the softness of her mouth. When the kiss ended, the strength of the yearning to claim her mouth once again blindsided him. As he acted on the impulse, she shoved him away.

"Hey." He steadied her as the force of her shove caused her to stumble. "Steady."

She touched a mouth that, to his immense satisfaction, looked ripe and very well kissed.

"I don't want this!"

Rafiq quelled the impulse to prove her passionately wrong. Instead, he arranged his features into an expression of concern. "There's nothing wrong with enjoying kissing one's future spouse."

"No." She shook her head. "That's just it. We're not getting married."

He smiled to mask the impatience that surged. He wanted her. He would have her—once they were married. He'd sate himself then cut her loose. But she need not know that yet.

"Let's not play games, Tiffany. Marriage was the

ultimate prize you hoped to secure by coming here. You say it wasn't about blackmail or money. So that leaves only marriage." His lip curled. "Well, *you've* gotten all you could ever have wanted."

"I don't want to marry you!"

"You came here because you wanted to marry someone else?" Rafiq's mocking retort was met with silence. His gaze narrowed. A lightning-fast glance took in the slender fingers clenched into fists, her wary, defiant eyes.

There was someone else.

A blaze of possessiveness roared through him, the need to stake his claim, to mark her as his, now and forever. He yanked her up against him, tangled his hands in the tumbled waves of hair and captured her mouth roughly with his.

He was aware of the fine tremors that shimmered through her, of the way his thigh fitted between hers and how the cradle of her hips rocked against him. The intoxicating scent and taste of her filled his senses, and her tongue danced with his.

He was aware of everything about her. Only her. The rest of the world receded.

He was so far gone, that he didn't care about control, about leashing it, about the fact that Dr. Farouk might walk back into her office and discover him alone with her, kissing her. There was just Tiffany…and him.

And she was going to marry him.

Only him.

He broke the kiss and set her away from him with shaking hands. "There," he said, making his point. "You can't possibly share what we have with any other man."

"I don't."

Confused, he shook his head. Had he imagined the

expression on her face? No, it had been there. A look of yearning—and it hadn't been for him. He narrowed his gaze in a way that anyone who knew him well recognized. "Where is this fool who allows you to roam the bars of Hong Kong alone, untended? Who leaves you vulnerable to other men?"

"I haven't met him yet."

"What?" Rafiq felt like the world had tipped upside down. "We're arguing over a man who does not even exist?"

"Oh, he does exist." She wore a dreamy expression. "I know he does. Otherwise why was I put on earth? He's out there somewhere. I couldn't believe in love as much as I do, and have it not happen." A shadow passed over her face. "But I can promise you one thing—he's nothing like you. Suspicious. Distrustful. Emotionless."

"So what's he like then?" he scoffed.

Her eyes had gone soft and dewy. "He's ordinary. He's not famous. Or wealthy. He doesn't live in an obscenely ornate home, nor does he have movie-star looks—"

He bowed his head, and said with irony, "Thank you."

"I'm not referring to you," she said crushingly. "I'm trying to explain how ordinary he is. A white picket fence and two-point-four children kind of guy."

"Then what makes him so special?"

"He'll love me," she said simply. "And I'm the most important person in his whole world. In fact, I am his world. There's none of the pomp and circumstance that fills your existence."

The red tide that crashed over him couldn't possibly be jealousy. By Allah, the man did not even exist. Incredulous, he glared at her. Rafiq gazed into her clear, desert-and-sunshine eyes. His chest tightened.

Tiffany was speaking the absolute truth. She didn't want him. She wanted someone else…someone he could never be.

Seven

Tiffany might have won the skirmish about having a DNA test done, but the tension that filled the back of the chauffeur-driven limousine as they left the doctor's office warned her that there were still plenty of battles to come.

Rafiq broke the silence that stretched between them by leaning forward to issue instructions in Arabic through the intercom to the chauffeur.

"Let's walk," Rafiq said abruptly, as the Mercedes-Benz came to a stop and the back doors opened.

Tiffany followed him out and caught her breath at the sight of the park that sprawled in front of them, tall trees shading open green lawns and a forest of roses beyond. "Where is this?"

"These are the botanical gardens that lie between the hospital and the university. They were laid out by one of my ancestors. She loved gardens and roses."

"It's beautiful. So green. So unlike anything I ever expected to find in a desert."

"The unexpected surprise surpasses the expected."

"Is that a proverb?" she asked, and for a moment there was absolute accord, a sense of intimacy between them, as their eyes met and he gave her a slight smile.

"No, it's original. You can claim it if you wish."

The awful tension that had started in the doctor's rooms began to ease. She smiled back at him. "What a wonderfully romantic place."

"Don't hope to find your dream man here." Rafiq's face grew taut. "You may as well accept you're going to marry me."

Biting her lip, Tiffany walked swiftly away from him and considered her options. Marriage to Rafiq would make her parents' marriage look like a picnic at Disneyland by comparison. But the set of his jaw warned Tiffany to tread carefully. He might not believe the child was his, but he feared the slur of illegitimacy. Rafiq had decided to keep the scandal—and her—within his control.

She'd reached the rose gardens. She halted beside a bed of pale pink flowers. Rafiq stopped beside her. "Rafiq, be reasonable—"

"I'm being perfectly reasonable." He tipped his head back, and gave her a particularly arrogant look.

She gave a little laugh of disbelief. "You don't even believe I'm carrying your child." She touched her stomach. "Yet you're prepared to marry me. That's reasonable?"

"You didn't want to do the tests necessary to establish the baby's paternity, and I didn't force you. I'm prepared to take your word that it's my child and marry you, so that the real truth can be determined once the baby is born—as you suggested. How can you possibly accuse me of being unreasonable?"

He wore such a fake-patient expression that Tiffany ground her teeth. How had he managed to twist it all to make her the unreasonable party here?

To temper her rising agitation, Tiffany sucked in a steadying breath and tried to let the soft, warm wind that blew over the rose beds, releasing their sweet scent, soothe her frayed nerves. "All I wanted was to make sure that my daughter had a right to know who her father was. And to find out whether you would be prepared to acknowledge her—if she feels the need to seek you out one day. I had hoped we could visit. When she's older," she added hastily as his brows shot up, "she'll want to know who her father is."

He inclined his head. "Of course. I should've expected this. You came here to have me sign some sort of acknowledgment of paternity. A document that would enable you to claim maintenance, too."

"Coming here was never about money!" Tiffany almost stamped her foot. This was not about his ego. Or hers. It was about their daughter.

He spread his hands. "It no longer matters, Tiffany. Marry me, then as soon as the child is born we can test for paternity. If she is mine, I will support her. It is my duty."

Money. Duty. Those were the reasons a man like Rafiq married. It wasn't the kind of marriage she wanted for herself. Nor had she ever intended to marry a man of his wealth and position. She'd seen the strain a high-profile lifestyle had placed on her parents' marriage—a show-biz union—not a royal wedding, and her father didn't even have the kind of power this man did.

"Marriage between us would be a mistake," she argued desperately.

Rafiq was arrogant—even more arrogant than her

father. Tiffany shivered. Her father had trampled all over her mother's feelings with little respect. Given that the man before her had been treated like a proper prince since the moment he'd been born, she could expect even less from Rafiq.

If she were foolish enough to marry him…

"Why should it be a mistake?" His frown cleared. "We will work on it. All marriages take work."

Tiffany goggled at him, unable to believe what she was hearing. "You're prepared to put *work* into our marriage?" That was more than her father had ever done.

For a moment he hesitated, then he smiled, a charming smile that, despite all her reservations, caused tiny electric quivers to shoot through her. "Of course, I will work at it," he assured her.

So what if she reacted to his smile? She wanted the man. No problems there. Her body adored him. Just as well she wasn't ruled by her senses. "You'll really work at it?"

Rafiq's gaze bored into her. "You don't believe me, do you?"

She shrugged. "I'm sure you have great intentions."

"Why?"

"Why what?"

"Why can't you believe me?"

Okay, so maybe she'd been wrong. Her gaze slid away from his. Maybe marriage to him would work for their child. But it was a big decision to make—probably the biggest decision of her life. A group of students dressed in denim and some in traditional dress sauntered past them, chatting and laughing.

Tiffany drew a deep breath, weighing up whether to confide in Rafiq what a dreadful mess her parents' marriage had been, then dismissed the impulse. Why would Rafiq care?

When she turned her attention back to him, it was to find that he'd moved. He stood before her now, blocking her way, formidable and intimidating.

"I'm prepared to marry you, Tiffany. What have you got to lose?"

He said it as though she should be grateful for his largesse. It irked her that he thought she'd be such a pushover. "I'm not quite the nobody you think. My father is Taylor Smith."

He didn't react to the name. Finally he shook his head. "Should I know him?"

"In some circles he's very well-known. He's a film director."

"A film director." He raised an eyebrow. "What kind of film director?"

"He doesn't make skin flicks, in case that's what you're thinking." His films might be respectable, but her father's private life was a different story. The scandals that followed him would not meet the approval of someone as upstanding as Rafiq. "He's quite successful. He directed *Legacy*." Tiffany named a film that had taken the world by storm a couple of years ago. Recognition lit Rafiq's eyes.

"I watched that movie on the jet—it was about two years ago."

"That must've been when it first came out." His casual reference to flying by jet made Tiffany realize that while her father might travel by jet as part of his work, this man owned one. Help, his family probably owned a fleet of Lear jets!

"If your father is wealthy and successful, why were you working in Le Club?" he was asking.

Tiffany braced herself to hold his gaze. "After my purse was stolen, I called home. I discovered my father had left my mother for another woman the day before I met you in Hong Kong."

A host of unidentifiable emotions flickered over his face. "That would've been a shock."

"It was," she agreed, reaching blindly past him to touch a full, pink bloom, to give herself something to do. The velvet smoothness of the petals under her fingertips steadied her as she stroked them. "But there was nothing I could do. I could hardly add to my mother's stress at the time by telling her about the fix I was in—or asking her for money she didn't have. And my father was nowhere to be found. Nor could I have his business manager arrange it—because that was who he chose to run off with."

"So that's why—" He broke off.

"That's why what?" she prompted, glancing up at him.

The bitter chocolate of his eyes had turned black. "You had no one you could ask for money."

"I would've gotten out of there."

"By continuing to work at Le Club…by selling your body?" He looked suddenly, murderously angry.

"No, I would never do that!"

"Okay, I shouldn't have implied that you would. But now I understand why you are so reluctant to marry me."

"What do you mean?"

"You don't trust any man not to let you down."

Tiffany forced herself not to flinch. "That's ridiculous! You expected me to leap on your proposal? To marry you without thinking it through?" At his glowering expression, she said, "Oh, you did! I can see it on your face. Rafiq, how arrogant!"

Dark brows lowered over his eyes. "But when you think it through, you'll realize that it's the best option you have open to you." Rafiq reached forward and plucked one perfect, pale pink bloom then handed it to her. "Think of the child. This way the baby starts its life with both its parents."

Clutching the stem, Tiffany bent her head and inhaled the fragrance of the flower.

Yes. Rafiq was right. She had to think about her baby. Not about herself, what she wanted, but what would be best for her baby. She'd wanted to give her daughter the chance to have a meaningful relationship with her father, unbroken by the estrangement of living in separate countries she'd had with her father growing up.

Rafiq was offering that.

Raising her head, Tiffany said, "I need time to marshal my thoughts. Let me think about your proposal."

"I have a function tonight. I can afford to give you one night." He gave her a slow, incredibly sexy smile that caused her heart to roll over. "But be warned, I will demolish every one of your objections."

The Mercedes swept out of the forecourt of his home, returning Rafiq to the bank for the meetings that lay ahead for the rest of the day. Uncharacteristically, instead of pulling out his laptop and busying himself with the necessary preparation, he leaned back against the butter-soft leather headrest and stared out the window.

Tiffany came from a family that had wealth—and, possibly connections. It should've delighted him. It certainly made it easier to present her to his father as his prospective bride. The king would relish the red-carpet connection. Instead Rafiq felt as though someone had claimed a private treasure, one that he'd prided himself on discovering and appreciating when no one else did, and exposed it to the world.

Of course, the revelation meant that Tiffany didn't need

his resources, his wealth—as he'd mistakenly believed. She had no need to marry him, except for the baby's sake. She didn't even particularly want to marry him....

It was a startling realization. And it changed everything. Because he wanted her, had no intention of letting her go—at least not yet, and certainly not because of some fairy-tale notion of love that she desired.

They had so much more. She'd woken a fire, a depth of passion, that he'd never suspected existed within himself. He intended to stoke that fire, feed the flames and experience the full blast of the heat.

Tiffany *would* marry him.

The extent of his determination astonished him. What had happened to the part of him that withdrew when his paramours wanted a commitment and his father demanded a wedding date be set? Where had the voice of reason gone that anxiously warned him to take a step back before he got boxed in and caged for life?

Perhaps it was silent because this time he had an escape hatch. He stared unseeingly at the streetscape, not noticing the busy market as the Mercedes cruised past. Tiffany had even sensed it when she'd expressed her doubts about his promise to work on their marriage. The solution that had seemed so crystal clear after his discussion with Khalid was starting to become murky.

Because of this desire she roused in him.

Rafiq tried to tell himself this want wouldn't last. By the time the baby was born, the desire would be spent. Then he would do as he'd intended. *If* the DNA tests proved the baby was a member of their family, he would keep the baby—and divorce Tiffany. He'd have done his duty. The baby would be legitimate. In terms of the marriage contracts, he'd settle a fair sum of money on Tiffany.

He'd support his child. Make sure it—he, Rafiq

amended—went to the right schools, was given a fitting education and upbringing. The fact that Tiffany's father had wealth was an inconvenience, but Rafiq had no doubt he had the resources, the power, to win any legal battle her family chose to mount to seize the child. He would start by having Taylor Smith investigated to find out exactly what kind of financial resources the man had, and whether he possessed an Achilles' heel.

If the baby wasn't his…?

The Mercedes slowed to turn into the bank's underground car park. Still he hadn't started up his laptop, opened his calendar to view his coming appointments. The conundrum of Tiffany held his full attention. Rafiq didn't even want to think about how he would feel if it had all been an elaborate lie, if the baby wasn't his.

If she'd lied to him—he'd make Tiffany rue the day they'd ever met.

The night was long. Tiffany barely slept. Restlessness had taken hold of her.

Yes?

Or no?

What answer to give Rafiq?

Tiffany rolled into a ball, huddling her belly, and stared blindly into the darkness. If she refused to marry him and left Dhahara, while her daughter would have a mother, she'd grow up never knowing her father. Then what if Rafiq wanted nothing to do with her baby later…when she was older? At least if she married Rafiq now, he'd see the baby every day. A bond would form. How could it not?

Did she really have a choice?

With a sigh Tiffany flopped over onto her back. The man she'd met again in Dhahara was every bit as arrow-straight as the first time she'd met him. Suppressing her anxieties that she might lose her child, she'd come to Dhahara to establish contact with a banker…and discovered a sheikh. A royal prince.

Rafiq was a busy man. An important man. Tiffany already knew he traveled extensively. Would he take time out to spend with a family he'd never wanted? A baby daughter who was not the male heir he expected? Or would it be a reenactment of her own childhood with a father who was never home?

Through the window she could see only the brightest stars sprinkling the darkness. The moon was fuller than the sliver that had hung in the sky the night her baby had been conceived. If she married Rafiq, she would be the moon to his sun…barely meeting and separated by vast chasms of yawning space.

That realization made the decision so much easier. She did not want that kind of marriage. She would refuse his offer of marriage, and take her chances alone. One day she would tell her daughter who her father was. They didn't need Rafiq to be a family.

The decision that had been tormenting her made, Tiffany finally drifted off to sleep.

Tiffany's decision to turn down Rafiq's proposal was reinforced the next morning when she went down to breakfast and Lily hastily closed the newspaper she'd been leafing through—but not before Tiffany had caught a glimpse of Rafiq's handsome features spread over the page.

"May I?" She gave Lily a grim smile and reached for the paper.

Lily must've seen something in her face because she spread her hands helplessly. "You must realize, it's not my nephew's fault—women have been throwing themselves at him since he was a teenager."

So much for Rafiq's explanation to his aunt that they were business acquaintances. Lily had clearly read much more into their relationship.

Yet Lily's words brought no comfort. Tiffany stared at a series of photos of Rafiq at what was obviously a society event, a beautiful dark-haired woman clinging to his arm. This was why he hadn't been home for dinner last night. He'd generously given her time to make her decision, while he'd escorted another woman to a function.

Most women think I'm charming.

It appeared Rafiq had been right.

"She's beautiful," said Tiffany expressionlessly, her stomach tightening into a hard knot. *So this is how it begins.* It was her father all over again. There would always be women. The knowledge hurt more than she'd ever thought it could.

"It's the opening of the new wing of the hospital. Her family is well-known in Dhahara—and I'm sure Rafiq allowed himself to be photographed with her because of the large donation her family made to the new wing."

That possessive hand on his sleeve was a world away from polite. The tilt of the woman's head, her kohl-outlined eyes and society-goddess smile all announced her confidence in securing the man beside her to the world. Tiffany had never wanted a high-profile man who attracted women like bees to a honeypot. She had no intention of enduring what her mother had put up with.

Marriage to Rafiq was her idea of hell on earth.

She was going to say no—not only because her daughter deserved more than an absentee father, but also because she wasn't prepared to tolerate a string of photos with women that caused her to feel sick with doubt. Now she just had to communicate her decision to Rafiq. No doubt, he'd be glad to be rid of her. By tonight she'd be gone.

Turning her head away from Lily's concerned glance, Tiffany helped herself to apricots and dates and spooned over creamy yogurt and honey, sure that if she tried to eat anything more substantial she would gag—despite the beautiful display.

By the time Rafiq strode in minutes later, the offending newspaper had been folded and tucked away. Yet not even the flash of his white smile and his warm greeting could bring any softening to Tiffany's resolve. Her stomach started to churn, and nausea rose in the back of her throat.

Her spoon clattered into her bowl, and Tiffany pushed her chair back.

"Not so fast," Rafiq's tone made her pause. "Stay. We must talk."

Lily glanced at him. "I've got a few calls to make. I'll make them in your study if you don't mind, Rafiq."

Tiffany wanted to scuttle after Lily, anything to avoid the coming unpleasantness. Then she stiffened her spine. She'd sit across the table from Rafiq and give him her answer.

The sooner she got it over with, the better.

"I have one thing to ask of you," Rafiq said after his aunt had left them alone, his voice pure liquid. He'd pulled a chair up beside her, turning it so that he was so close that she could inhale the scent of lemon and soap.

Jolted out of her thoughts, Tiffany stared at him.

"We will create a tale of how we met. No one need ever know of our ignominious start. We will keep to the story that we are business acquaintances…who met during your time at university."

"You mean lie?"

He ignored her angry comment. "You did go to university, didn't you?"

He hadn't asked her that in Hong Kong. "I studied English literature and French. Our paths were unlikely to have crossed."

"You speak French?"

She nodded.

"Good," he said. "We will say that you assisted me with some translation."

He was sweeping her objections aside. Tiffany knew she had to make a stand, before he walked all over her. "I haven't said I'll marry you."

"Oh, we both know what your final answer will be. I only want to whitewash our meeting so that our families are not hurt by the scandalous nature of our first encounter."

Her father was far from an angel. And once Rafiq discovered Taylor Smith's affairs, he'd be trying to protect his family from the taint of her father's reputation. "Now that you know my family is wealthy, you're obviously no longer worried that I might blackmail you and Sir Julian," she said with a bite in her voice, the memory of the image of him and the beautiful woman still burning like salt in a raw wound.

He shook his head. And her heart leaped. Then he killed the hope. "The deal with Sir Julian has already been announced. It can no longer be jeopardized."

Already hurting with an emotion she didn't want to label for fear of admitting what she dared not confront, it stung that he hadn't admitted that he'd been wrong to doubt her.

"I'm not going to marry you," she said baldly.

There was a silence.

"I beg your pardon?" His voice turned ominously soft. To her relief he made no move to shift closer.

"I can't marry you."

As Taylor Smith's daughter, Tiffany was every bit as unsuitable as a blackmailing club hostess he'd met one night in Hong Kong. Her father might be a film director, but Tiffany had no doubt that his list of affairs had made him too scandalous for Rafiq's conservative family to tolerate.

He raised a brow. "You must marry me."

"The only reason for our marriage is to legitimize the daughter you're not even convinced is yours." It irked her to remind him of that, but right now she needed every argument she could muster.

"The DNA tests will tell the truth when the time comes." He reached out and took her hand. "But you're mistaken, Tiffany. The baby is far from the only reason I have for desiring to marry you," he argued, his eyes glowing with a light she was starting to recognize.

Oh, no!

Tiffany tried to free her hand, waving the other to ward him off. But when he trailed a finger down the side of her face, little quivers of delight followed in its wake. "Rafiq, that's not going to work," she said rather breathlessly.

"This always works for us."

Not today. Jealousy mushroomed into rage. "You haven't seen the photos in today's paper."

"What, a photo of me with the daughter of a man who donated to a cause I am a founding patron for?"

"It didn't look that innocent."

"Her hand was on my arm. I did not touch her. Pah, that's the paparazzi—always on the lookout for a scandal."

There was a ring of truth in his impatience.

But Tiffany had learned young that there was no whiff of smoke without a raging inferno someplace. A picture of her father with an adoring starlet in the gossip rags usually escalated into a passionate affair with the young actress in question not long after.

And Rafiq had admitted the first night they met that women found him charming. She had been warned.

Turning in her chair, Tiffany pulled the newspaper out from where she'd tucked it away on the seat beside her and unfolded it, spreading it out on the table, to glance at the image again.

She stared hard. Rafiq was facing into a camera, his expression carefully blank. No smile for the woman at his side. No glow of romance. Was Rafiq really different from her father? She wanted desperately to believe he was, but she had no intention of fooling herself that she could change such a man.

Perhaps the woman in the newspaper was indeed no more than a woman whose family he knew, a family who had donated a large sum to a good cause he sponsored.

She set the paper aside.

Rafiq was watching her. He hadn't even spared the paper a glance—he obviously didn't care what she believed. The ache in her chest that had begun when she'd first seen that picture intensified. It was an ache that was starting to concern her greatly.

"Have you ever been in love?" she asked suddenly.

"The kind of love that the poets wail about?" Rafiq grimaced. "Probably not. But the kind of love that makes me desire a woman? Then yes, several times—with a number of highly suitable women."

His candor caused a fresh stab of sharper pain.

Well, she'd asked, hadn't she? She could hardly complain when she didn't like the reply.

Shoring up optimism, she said, "But you never married any of them."

"I considered marrying one or two."

Tiffany blinked. "You did? So what stopped you?"

He shrugged, then glanced away, his lashes falling to mask his unfathomable eyes. His hair shone in the light of the morning sun that streamed through the high windows above and into the dining room. "The pressure of expectation. I only had to show a small amount of interest in a woman for my family, her family and the newspapers to start setting wedding dates."

His honesty startled her. She wished she'd never asked. "You felt trapped."

He met her gaze squarely. "Yes."

"Yet you have asked me to marry you—demanded that I marry you, in fact. After what you just told me, how do I know you're not going to back out at the last moment if you start to feel pressured?"

"I *have* to marry you," he pointed out. "You are with child—my child, you assure me." Then he smiled, his eyes crinkling, and her breath snagged in her throat. "And, at this stage, you have the advantage that your father hasn't produced marriage agreements for me to sign."

"And I'm supposed to be relieved by that?"

He laughed.

Tiffany didn't.

It was starting to occur to her that she had a much bigger problem on her hands than she'd ever dreamed. The man who'd asked her to marry him had been caught by the oldest trick in the book: pregnancy. And, worse, he was every bit as terrified of being trapped as she was of being cheated on.

"Do you expect a marriage of convenience?" he asked.

She did a double take. "You mean no sex?"

Rafiq was a passionate man. Their night together had proved that beyond a shadow of doubt. She wouldn't have picked him for a man who could survive the sexless wasteland that a marriage in name only would be. Unless he planned to go to other women…despite his marriage vows. The ache inside her intensified.

With a firm shake of her head, she said, "I don't know why I said that. It's irrelevant. I don't want the kind of marriage we'd have."

"Then we can have a different kind of marriage." His eyes grew lazy and he tugged the hand that he was holding, propelling her closer. Her chair scraped across the highly polished wooden floor. "With lots of sex."

"That's not what I meant—"

Before she could finish setting him right, his mouth closed over hers, full of ardor. Tiffany tasted coffee and desire. Deliciously tempting. She edged nearer. Closing her eyes, she sagged against him.

His body was hard against hers. He was aroused, she realized. She pulled away. "No!" Her voice was sharp. "I don't want that kind of marriage, either."

"You might think a marriage of convenience would work for the child's sake. You might think you want a romantic fairy tale." His eyes had darkened, coal-black, piercing. "But what I'm offering is the exactly the kind of marriage you want."

She wrenched herself out of his arms. "You don't know me. You have no idea what I want!"

His lips curved up, and his eyes smoldered. "Then why don't you tell me exactly what you want, and I will do everything in my power to give it to you."

Little frissons of excitement ran up and down her spine. It annoyed her that he could control her body's response so easily. "I've told you before—I don't want *you*. I want to marry a different kind of man altogether, someone—"

"Ordinary." The sexy smile vanished. "You're chasing

a chimera, Tiffany. Maybe you even believe it, but one day you will discover what I know already—that you have deceived yourself. You do not want anyone ordinary."

Tiffany pushed her chair back and rose to her feet. Forcing herself to laugh, the kind of light, careless laugh her mother gave when she pretended to dismiss her father's flirtations as inconsequential, she said, "So I suppose you're going to tell me exactly what kind of man I do want?"

"You want *me*."

Eight

As his stark words disappeared into a void of resounding silence, Rafiq knew at once he'd been far too forthright. Honeyed sentiments about love were what women wanted, not the honest, unvarnished truth.

Tiffany looked shaken. She opened her mouth, then closed it again. At last she found her voice. "Your arrogance knows no bounds."

Heat expanded inside his chest. "Have you forgotten where the conversation ended up last time you called me an arrogant jerk?" he asked softly, getting to his feet.

By the golden fire in her eyes he saw that she remembered. Perfectly.

"It won't end up in the same place this time."

He cocked an eyebrow, and gave her a slow smile as he advanced. "You are certain of that?"

"Absolutely!"

"I relish a challenge." And he watched the dismay dawn on her face with masculine satisfaction.

"Wait…" Tiffany backed up until the table was behind her. She held up her hands. "I didn't mean for you to interpret my statement that you were arrogant as a challenge to get me back into your bed—"

"You agree it will be too easy?" He kept coming, until her hands were flat against his chest. Could she feel the thud of his heart against her palms? He was intensely aware of the touch of her fingers through the silk of his shirt.

"Definitely not."

Despite his growing arousal, Rafiq was starting to enjoy himself. He suppressed a grin. "And that is a challenge for me to prove how easy it will be?"

She did a double take.

"No! I mean—" She paused, clearly fearful that he'd taken her denial as a fresh challenge.

"Hush." He placed a finger against her lips. "It's why I'm such a good negotiator."

This time he allowed himself a smug grin.

Her retort was cut off by the appearance of an aide at the door. "Your Highness, your office called. The first appointment for the day has arrived."

Rafiq glanced down at his watch. He had no intention of telling Tiffany that Sir Julian had arrived in Dhahara, not while he was trying to convince her to marry him. "He is early. My secretary is away. Please let Miss Turner, her assistant, know I will be in shortly."

After the aide had left, all teasing humor faded. Leaning forward he said, "Tiffany, what happened between you and me that night in Hong Kong—" Rafiq caught her hand in his "—should never have happened. It was dishonorable."

She stared levelly back at him. "I've got as much to lose

as you—I have no intention of telling the paparazzi about our night together…or the life we created."

Rafiq threaded his fingers through hers, aware of the quiver of her fingers. "I'm relieved to hear that." She opened her mouth to object. He continued quickly, "That night should never have happened. I don't know why—" He broke off and shook his head.

He still didn't understand what had happened to him that night. How he'd lost control so fast. Why it lingered in his mind…tempting him to repeat the experience, to the point where he couldn't wait to marry Tiffany and get her back into his bed.

Finally he said, "It doesn't change the fact that I will take responsibility for my actions."

She glanced up sharply. "Are you saying that you're prepared to believe that the baby is yours?"

Rafiq shook his head slowly. "I do not say that." *Yet.* "But I am prepared to concede that it is possible, and for that reason I am prepared to marry you."

"Even though it makes you feel trapped?"

He hesitated, then decided to let her believe it. He'd already told her he wanted her. She didn't need to know the full extent of the sexual power she held over him. He thought of her every waking moment. He'd never experienced anything like it. What harm would it do to let her think he was marrying her only out of duty? "We will discover the truth when the baby is born. Until then we will not talk of this again. It is about time you met my family, don't you think?" He smiled at her. "I will arrange for them to gather at Qasr Al-Ward, my brother's home—I think you will like it there."

Her eyes widened. "Wait—you can't drop a bombshell like that and leave."

"I'll answer your questions later."

Rafiq raised her hand and kissed the back. She gasped. It seemed as if he wasn't the only one affected by the sensual tie that bound them.

"If I don't leave now, I will be late for my appointment. I will send a car for you at five o'clock. Be ready. Tonight we will plan our wedding."

Rafiq had spoken the truth.

Tiffany lay in the marble bath with its dolphin faucets, soaking to relax her aching neck muscles, and admitted the truth to herself. She'd been fooling herself, she wanted him, only him. Only he had ever aroused an emotion that she could label possessiveness. Only Rafiq had ignited the heat within her that made her melt when he was near her.

She'd come to Dhahara to build a bridge to the future for her unborn daughter. She'd discovered a man she was no longer sure she would be able to walk away from.

So why didn't she throw caution to the wind and marry him? Because she still clung to part of her dream. She wanted more than a father for her child, and a lover for herself.

She wanted a man to marry her not because she was pregnant, not because she carried a royal heir, but because he loved her. But that dream was the biggest fairy tale of all.

The reality was that once Rafiq discovered how much the tabloids stalked her fickle father, it would outweigh the scandal of an illegitimate heir being born into the royal family. It was unlikely that he would need any second urging to drop her like a hot potato.

Sir Julian Carling had an agenda.

Rafiq sensed it as soon as the other man greeted him

as he stepped into the bank's wood-paneled boardroom. As soon as the discussions about the new hotel were out the way, Sir Julian pounced.

"My daughter, Elizabeth, was very taken with you, Rafiq."

Rafiq could barely recall the debutante he'd met at Sir Julian's home months ago. Across the wooden boardroom table, he gave the older man a noncommittal smile and put his slimline laptop back in its case. "I'm sure any man would be flattered by her attention."

Sprawled in the leather-backed chair, Julian said, "She's coming to Dhahara—the only reason she didn't come with me now is a work commitment. She's very involved in the Carling Hotel group, but she'd like to get to know you better. Perhaps, once Elizabeth arrives, we can talk about building a second hotel in one of the desert cities."

It was a bribe.

Rafiq had not managed to remain unwed for more than three decades without developing an uncanny sixth sense about matchmaking parents. But this time he got the feeling that he was being craftily boxed in by a master operator. Getting to his feet, he made it clear that the meeting was at an end. "Julian, I must inform you that I'm getting married. My bride and I will probably be away when your daughter arrives."

"Married?" Sir Julian sat up and planted his elbows on the boardroom table, displeasure written all over his florid features. "When I spoke to your father only a few days ago, he suggested I bring Elizabeth to spend time with you. He said nothing about your marriage."

Because, at the time, his crafty father hadn't known. Rafiq could have throttled the king. So much for taking up his joking suggestion that Elizabeth Carling might suit Khalid; his father had had another plan altogether.

"My bride and I will be married before the week is out." Speaking with utmost confidence, Rafiq bent to pick up his laptop case. He would give Tiffany—and the king—no choice in the matter. She'd become a temptation he could not withstand.

"I'll have to make sure I'm here to celebrate the event."

"My fiancée wants a quiet, family wedding." As he spoke, Rafiq wondered whether Tiffany would agree to a marriage without her parents present to give their blessing.

Tiffany didn't know what she'd expected, but it certainly wasn't the fortress of sun-bleached sandstone that rose out the surrounding desert. She peered through the window of the Mercedes-Benz to get a better look.

"Good heavens."

"Qasr Al-Ward," Rafiq announced as the black car came to a stop in the graveled forecourt.

"Your brother and his wife live here?"

"Yes, my brother has made his home here—he spends as much time as he can away from the city with his wife."

Only one wife?

But Tiffany bit back the sarcastic retort as the chauffeur opened the door for her. The stifling heat of the late afternoon closed around her. Alighting from the backseat, she started to worry about the simple white dress she wore. "I'm not dressed up enough."

"Don't worry. More often than not Shafir is covered in desert sand. My brother won't even notice what you are wearing." There was a gleam of humor in Rafiq's eyes. "But if what you are wearing concerns you, I am sure clothes can be found that will be more to your liking."

Shafir Al Dhahara wore flowing white robes with not

a speck of dust. But his wife was a surprise. Tiffany found herself enchanted by Megan—and it was clear that Shafir adored his wife.

"I have heard all about you," said a tall, dark man with liquid-gold eyes coming up to stand behind the couple at the top of the stone stairs that led to the vast front door. "Rafiq, aren't you going to introduce us?"

Well, Tiffany had heard nothing about him—she didn't even know who he was.

Rafiq waved a careless hand. "Tiffany, this is my brother, Khalid."

She smiled, and wondered how many more brothers Rafiq had.

As if Khalid had read her thoughts, he said, "There are three of us. I am the eldest and Shafir here is the middle son. Rafiq is the baby of the family."

Ha. Some baby!

Tiffany waited for Rafiq to object; instead he gave his brother a rough hug. "Father will be here later. He had a meeting with the council of elders. Now let us go inside."

The thought of meeting Rafiq's father, the king, was enough to give Tiffany the shakes. But before she could worry about it any further, Shafir's wife came up beside her.

"Would you like something to drink?" Megan asked. "It's going to be a hectic few hours."

A hectic few hours?

Despite her bemusement Tiffany requested a glass of soda.

"What did Megan mean by 'a hectic few hours'?" she asked, dropping back to speak to Rafiq.

He avoided her gaze.

She put a hand on his arm to stop him moving away. "Answer me."

"Ah, look at the lovebirds," chortled Shafir.

"Let Tiffany and Rafiq alone," Megan scolded her husband. "Rafiq, you can use your usual suite of rooms. Tiffany, for now, I've given you a chamber in the old harem—but don't let that freak you out."

Megan's statement did indeed freak her out. But not the bit about the harem. "A chamber?"

Did Megan mean a bedchamber? They weren't staying the night, were they? Rafiq had said nothing about that.

Megan nodded. "I'll send one of the maids to help you dress for the party."

Help her dress? Tiffany suddenly knew exactly how Alice must've felt when she blundered down the rabbit hole. "What party? I didn't think to bring a change of clothes with me."

"Your clothes—"

"Megan," her husband grasped her arm, "you talk too much."

Megan glanced around, a resigned expression on her face. "Have I put my foot in it again?"

Turning away from his family to confront a silent Rafiq, Tiffany demanded, "What is going on?"

Behind her she could hear Megan saying, "Dammit, I *have* put my foot in it. Why did none of you bother to tell me that she didn't know?"

Tiffany's sense of ire grew. "Don't know what?"

"Er—" Rafiq started to move past her. "Come through to the salon."

"Rafiq?" She grabbed at his sleeve. "Tell me."

"My family—every one—is here to celebrate our engagement this evening."

Tiffany's mouth fell open. *"Our engagement?"*

"You should've tried seduction, Rafiq." The male voice was followed by hoots of laughter.

Oh, dear God! "Do they know I'm pregnant?" she whispered, humiliation creeping over her in a sickly wave at the thought of their night together being the subject of ridicule.

A flare of color seared his cheekbones, but he didn't drop his gaze. "Ignore Shafir, he knows nothing. It's a joke—I once told him he should seduce Megan—he's simply trying to score points."

"Did he?" she asked in a low tone.

"By your expression, it looks like he did."

She shook her head impatiently. "Not now. Did he seduce Megan?"

"No, he decided to kidnap her instead."

"Kidnap her?" Tiffany's eyes stretched wide as they followed the rest of the party into a large room that overlooked lush gardens with tall palms and pools of water. *"Really?"*

He nodded. "He brought her here—and kept her under lock and key."

"You've got to be joking! Right?"

Rafiq shook his head. "No, I'm not. Ask Megan."

Megan's voice piped up, "What must Tiffany ask me?"

"Hush, wife," said Shafir, and everyone laughed.

"Did your husband kidnap you?" Tiffany stared at the other woman, sure that she was being mercilessly teased.

"Oh, yes. Except he wasn't my husband back then."

"And he kept you here until you agreed to marry him?"

Megan shook her head, and reached for Shafir's hand before casting him a loving glance. "He didn't force me to marry him—he was trying to stop me from marrying Zara's fiancé."

"Zara's fiancé?" Tiffany did a double take. "But Zara's Lily's daughter. Isn't she in L.A.?"

Shafir only laughed. "It's a long story."

"Sounds like one I should hear," Tiffany said darkly.

"Not before you marry me," objected Rafiq. "Although maybe I'll have to take a leaf out of Shafir's book and lock you up here."

She spun around. *"What?"*

Rafiq glanced at her annoyed face and then around at their attentive audience. "Excuse us, please."

He wrapped one arm around her shoulders, hooked the other behind her knees and swept her off her feet. He hoisted her high against his chest. Tiffany buried her face against his throat to drown out the whoops of laughter as he exited the room.

When they reached a sitting room where scimitars adorned a wall, he lowered her to her feet.

Tiffany couldn't restrain herself. "How could you do that? *In front of your family?* And how could you announce our engagement to them? I haven't even said I'll marry you."

His eyes were guarded. "Of course you will."

Tiffany threw her hands up. "But I haven't said 'yes.'"

He arched a brow in a gesture that had become endearingly familiar. "So say it."

After seeing how Shafir doted on Megan, Tiffany was wildly tempted to give in and let herself be dragged down the aisle. When she'd come to Dhahara to tell Rafiq about his baby, marriage was not what she'd expected. Yet she was unbearably tempted.

A pang pierced her.

"Don't look so desperate."

She lifted her head. "I'm not desperate."

"Only love makes you desperate." His mouth twisted. "And this match isn't about love."

He paused, and Tiffany wondered how he expected her to respond. When he remained silent, she said, "You will regret our marriage."

"What do you mean?"

This time there was no hesitation. It wasn't right to let him walk into a marriage without at least warning him. "The tabloids adore my father. He can always be relied on to deliver a story."

"Do you mean that he feeds them Hollywood leaks?"

"No, no. Nothing like that. He has affairs with actresses—much to my mother's grief." She clenched her hands at her sides. "Your family will not be happy."

"Tiffany." His hands closed over her shoulders. He pulled her up against his chest. He felt so unabashedly solid and male. "You need to understand that I am marrying you—not your father."

"He will cause you a lot of embarrassment."

Rafiq shrugged against her. "That is not your doing."

The last bastion of her line of defense crumbled. A warmth spread through her, and tears pricked at her eyes. Her hands crept up his shirt front and a fierce emotion shook her.

"Thank you," she whispered.

What did she have to lose? Pulling back a little, Tiffany met his melting gaze, and said, "Okay, I'll marry you."

Nine

The wedding contracts had been signed.

Once Tiffany had accepted his proposal, Rafiq had wasted no time in the week that followed to arrange their wedding.

He thought about their unborn child. His daughter perhaps…

How would he have felt if some stranger had gotten his daughter pregnant after a one-night stand? Rafiq realized he would've been furious!

With a little trepidation he'd approached inviting her parents, but Tiffany had decided against it. Her mother had a lot of adjusting to do, she'd explained, and right now she didn't feel like seeing her father.

Rafiq hadn't agreed, but he'd gone along with it. For Tiffany's peace of mind.

Now, oblivious of the knot of people clustered around, Rafiq waited beside the ancient well in the heart of Ain

Farrin, the village not far from Qasr Al-Ward where the spring, or *ain,* originated, and watched Tiffany come toward him through the grove of tamarisk trees.

His bride.

She wore a long, cream-colored silk dress embroidered with rich gold thread and topped with a gauzy silk wrap. A filmy veil covered her hair. Her hips swayed as she walked, a legacy of the high heels she wore.

Rafiq wasn't aware of his family, or the villagers who crowded around. He only had eyes for Tiffany.

Her eyes glittered beneath the draped veil. She stopped beside him in the dappled shade of an ancient olive tree, and he reached for her hands. Her fingers trembled as his fingers closed around hers.

His bride was nervous.

Tenderness flowed through Rafiq. An urge to protect her from anything that might harm her. He drew her toward him and turned to face the celebrant.

He closed his eyes as the holy words flowed over them. After placing a ring on her finger, he received one in return. They knelt, then circled the well in a train, while the village children tossed rose petals from the gardens of Qasr Al-Ward over them.

As he brushed the petals from her veil, he saw her eyes were dazed.

"Almost over," he mouthed, and his heart soared as he caught a glimpse of her smile through the spun-silk veil.

He would not let her down, he vowed. Nor would he ever abandon their daughter when she needed him most.

After the wedding festivities were over, they returned to Qasr Al-Ward. Rafiq had told Tiffany that Shafir and Megan had loaned them the ancient palace for a few days.

The knowledge that, with the exception, of a skeleton staff, they were totally alone, made her unaccountably edgy.

Rafiq was her husband.

They were married.

She was already expecting his daughter; this was not going to be the romantic honeymoon of newlyweds.

Yet as the sun sank over the distant horizon, leaving a glow of burnished gold over the desert sands, Tiffany followed Rafiq through corridors lit by torches set in wall sconces, and couldn't help being affected by the expectant air of exotic romance. It felt like a honeymoon. Blood pounded through her veins.

When he led her into a vast chamber lit by dozens of candles that illuminated a bed in the center, she balked.

"What about our marriage of convenience?"

That got his attention. He swiveled to face her. "It's not going to happen. I made that clear when I asked if you expected one. I know you, Tiffany, better than you think. I suspected you might have convinced yourself that was what you want."

"But you knew better."

The candlelight gave his skin a bronze cast. It threw warmth over the harsh features, and lit up the white pants and tunic he'd worn for their marriage. "I know what you want. You want me."

The bed behind him loomed large in the room. Tiffany could already feel that her breathing had quickened, that her body had softened. "You flatter yourself."

His mouth slanted. "Because I can never be the white knight of your dreams?"

The edge to his voice caused her to frown.

"Exactly."

"You're fooling yourself if you think you can exist

without passion. You were made to make love. I knew that the first night we were together."

Determined not to fall into his arms, she said, "I only slept with you out of gratitude."

His eyes began to glitter. "Did you?"

Her pulse accelerated and she crossed her fingers. "Yes."

"Thirty dollars worth of gratitude?"

She didn't like the way he made that sound. "Uh…"

"And this time you're sleeping with me because you're so grateful—" he stressed the word as he stalked toward her "—that I married you?"

"Of course not!"

She didn't back away as he came to a halt in front of her. "Then it must be because you know exactly how much pleasure is in store for you, hmm?"

Her stomach started to flutter. "No, Rafiq, no sex."

Not now. Not while he was in this mood, even though she knew she'd deliberately provoked him.

"It will be much more than sex." His voice deepened to a husky growl that turned knots in her stomach. "I will pleasure you, just you wait and see."

He planted his mouth on hers and her lips parted.

It didn't take long for him to elicit a response, even though Tiffany fought with herself to resist. To her utter frustration he raised his head just enough to put a space between them. "Are you suitably grateful for that?"

The high heels she wore meant her eyes were level with the sinful passion of his mouth.

"Just shut up," she said, flustered by the desire that bolted through her like a jab of electricity.

This time, when he took her in his arms, she went up on the tips of her toes, and met him halfway. All her objections had evaporated.

"You know I'll never forgive you for this, don't you?" she muttered when he lowered her to the soft satin covers.

He laughed as he slipped off her shoes. "I've been wanting to do that all day." Next he peeled off the veil and carefully eased the ivory and gold dress away from her shoulders.

He followed her down onto the bed. "You'll love every moment. That I will promise you."

When she woke the next morning it was to meet a pair of slumberous dark eyes. Embarrassment seared Tiffany. Her cheeks grew hot, her breasts, the heat spread.

Rafiq propped himself onto an elbow and started to smile as he gazed down at her. His eyes glowed. "You don't need to blush—we have done nothing to be ashamed of. We are married."

She gave an incoherent murmur.

He pushed the sheet away from her body. Tiffany snatched at the edge as it slipped away.

"Don't be shy." His hand stroked the soft flesh of her stomach. "I find it hard to believe there is a baby in here. You were so tight… You could've been a virgin."

Tiffany's flush deepened. "You're embarrassing me," she said.

"Why?" At her sharp inhalation, he said, "Let's have no pretense or secrets between us, Tiffany. I knew you were no virgin last night."

Her breath whooshed out in a frustrated sigh. "If there are to be no secrets, then you should know that the only other time we made…love—" she stumbled over the word "—I was a virgin."

Tiffany glanced up at him from beneath her eyelashes to see how he'd taken her revelation.

His face had gone curiously blank. After a moment's

pause, he said, "Ah, Tiffany, you need not worry. I did not expect to find an innocent that night we first met."

She fell silent, her lashes sweeping down against her cheeks.

"Do not sulk," he whispered, running a finger along the ridge of her nose. "I never wanted a virgin."

Her lashes lifted. She met his eyes, so close now, that a stab of desire spiked through her. "I'm not sulking! But I had hoped you'd gotten to know me better by now. That first night in Hong Kong, you thought I was scamming you—"

"I know—"

"I was in a desperate situation—"

"I know that—"

"I've repaid every cent you gave me. I've told you the truth about the baby—"

"Tiffany, Tiffany." He pulled her into his arms and rolled onto his back, tugging her over on top of his chest. "It doesn't matter whether you were a virgin or not." He lifted his head off the pillow and kissed her brow.

She opened her mouth to tell him that it did matter. That she needed him to trust her—as she'd trusted him by telling him about her parents, by confessing that her father would never be the ideal father-in-law. She needed a show of faith from him, too. And more than anything, she needed for him to believe that the baby was his. Just because she said so.

Not because of the incontrovertible results of a DNA test.

It hurt, this refusal to trust her. But he would learn that she hadn't lied to him—then he would be forced to apologize.

"Stop glowering at me." He ruffled her hair. "We will

make love. Then I will show you the desert that has always been so loved by my family."

Just as she had no doubt he intended, desire started to sing through her veins.

What did Rafiq love? Was it only sex? Would he ever love more than the attraction that burned so brightly, so wildly between them?

At that thought her heart thudded to a stop. Was this the reason she so desperately needed for him to trust her? Had she fallen in love with the husband she'd trapped into a marriage that he'd entered only from a sense of duty?

"Mom?" Tiffany pressed the telephone against her ear to overcome the hiss on the line. "How are you?"

"Holding together. I signed the final settlement papers yesterday—your father wasn't there."

Was that a wistful note she heard in her mother's voice? Tiffany fervently hoped not.

"Everything went smoothly," Linda Smith continued, "just as you said it would once we got a good lawyer."

"I'm glad." Tiffany gave a silent sigh of relief. Two months ago she'd found her mother a lawyer, and she'd gone with her to every appointment and provided moral support right up to the day before she'd left for Dhahara. With the settlement signed, at last her mother could start to put together the pieces of her life. "Have you thought any more about selling the house in Auckland and finding something cozier?"

Before Tiffany had left, her mother had still been adamant that she didn't want to move out of the house she'd shared with Taylor Smith—even though it was the best asset she owned. Tiffany had suspected her mother was clutching at straws, hoping her father would come to his senses and return.

How Linda could consider taking him back this time, when he'd physically moved out, Tiffany found hard to figure.

"No, I don't want to sell—and you'll need somewhere to stay when you come back from your holiday. Where was it you were going again?"

"Dhahara. Mom, there's something I need to tell you." Tiffany plunged on. "I'm not coming home for a while. I got married."

She held the handset away as her mother gasped, then squealed and reeled off a string of questions.

"I know it was sudden. But it was the right thing to do. His name is Rafiq…and the marriage was performed in a village near one of the family's homes. Three days ago."

This time her mother sounded more cautious than celebratory. "Three days ago? In that desert country?"

"Yes, Dhahara is a desert kingdom." Then, hoping it would reassure her mother, she added, "Rafiq is part of the royal family."

"Oh, honey, you will come visit?"

Tiffany's heart ached at the loneliness in her mom's voice. "Of course, we'll come see you. Rafiq travels a great deal—he's a banker. We'll visit soon. I'll talk to him, and let you know when."

"Tiffany…are you sure you're all right? It's such a long way away. I wish I could be there to help you."

"I'm fine. Honestly. You're better off selling the house than rushing across the world to see me."

Her mother sighed. "I don't want to move. And I feel I should be with you. I wish your father were here. He'd know what to do."

"I haven't told Dad about my marriage."

Tiffany heard her mother's intake of breath.

"But he's your father—he has a right to know."

"I will tell him, Mom." Eventually. "Right now I'm still too angry with him for walking out on you." And her father was equally stubborn—he hadn't contacted her since their stormy disagreement when he'd cut off her allowance, and told her that she'd be back soon enough with her tail between her legs.

"Tiffany, it's not your fight. With the counseling I started, I'm working on forgiving your father, and I'm starting to realize I may not have been the best wife."

"Oh, no, Mom—don't even think that! He had no reason to run around with other women. To walk out on you."

Silence hummed between them. At last her mother said, "But you need to let him know about your marriage. You're still his baby girl."

It had been a long time since she'd been his little girl. Tiffany gentled her tone. "When I'm ready—I'm not ready yet." More than anything in the world she needed time.

"Darling, are you sure you know what you're—"

"I'm expecting Rafiq's baby, Mom."

This time the silence was electric.

To break it, Tiffany said desperately, "I came to Dhahara to tell Rafiq about the baby. My little girl will need a mother *and* a father." Surely her mother, of all people, would understand that better than anyone in the world? "In time she'll need grandparents, too, so don't worry. I know I have to tell Dad the good news."

Just not now. Not while her own hurt at his countless betrayals would spill out.

"Oh, darling, you should've told me you were pregnant before you left."

Tiffany couldn't handle recriminations right now. "Mom, you had enough to cope with."

"I feel terrible. I didn't even guess—"

"You weren't supposed to."

There was a short pause as her mother absorbed that. Then she said, "I feel like I let you down."

"Nonsense," said Tiffany loyally.

"But—"

"Don't worry about me," Tiffany interrupted. "I'm fine, Mom. I needed to make this decision myself. No one else could make it for me. Not you. Not Dad. Only I can take responsibility for my actions. I went into this with my eyes wide open."

That wasn't strictly true. She'd gone in with some illusions. She hadn't expected their marriage to be so *physical*. She was terrified of losing her emerging sense of identity to the heady passion that only Rafiq had ever awoken in her.

And now he was her husband...

The man who shared her bed. Her body. His body. Every night.

At least she wasn't in love with him. Nor he with her. It was better that way. Falling for Rafiq would be insanely stupid. Tiffany was not about to let Rafiq break her heart— not even if she was pregnant with his baby.

But she couldn't share any of that with her mother. Instead she said, "Rafiq took me into the desert yesterday. Oh, Mom, it was so beautiful.... One day I will show you, too."

Then maybe her mother might understand.

Ten

Rafiq gazed down at his wife.

A heavy tide of satisfaction swept in the wake of the rush of desire. They'd made love…slept…then made love again as dawn streaked the horizon.

He should've been sated.

He wasn't.

It would be a long time before he could claim to have had enough of his wife. But he would wait for tonight before taking her again. The day was hers. He would let anticipation build through the long, hot hours. Take her to a souk to watch her touch the soft silks. For an outing in the desert to see the excited glow in her eyes. He'd take her anywhere she chose to go. It was refreshing to see his world—Dhahara—through her eyes. The want could wait.

Until tonight.

"What would you like to do today?" He walked two fingers along her arm.

She peeped at him from beneath her eyelashes in a way that caused his heart to hammer in his chest. "It's been a very busy week."

"Indeed it has been," he agreed huskily.

"Is it going to be as hot today as it was yesterday?"

"Hotter."

She pursed her lips, her expression thoughtful. Her lashes fluttered down against her cheeks. "Perhaps we could stay here."

"Perhaps we should."

A wanton warmth pooled in the pit of his belly. Rafiq could think of nothing more perfect than remaining exactly where they were—here in this bedchamber, the lacy white wooden shutters flung open to the whisper of the desert wind.

Tiffany was fitting surprisingly well into his life. His aunt Lily had taken a shine to her—probably because she was missing Zara. His brothers liked her. He was sure his father had enjoyed meeting her, too, although they had spoken only briefly the night of their engagement and at the wedding.

As for him…

He thought Tiffany was everything he'd ever wanted. Reaching out one hand, he pushed the curtain of silken hair off her face, then leaned down and pressed a kiss against her cheek. It was an impulsive gesture, done without plan. Yet she immediately turned her head and her lips clung to his in a kiss so gentle, so full of sweetness, that his chest grew tight.

He groaned softly.

He had intended to break the news of Tiffany's pregnancy to his family. To confess the real reason for their marriage. So that they knew that after the birth of the child the marriage could be dissolved. Yet somehow he'd kept putting it off. And now he couldn't very well announce she was pregnant—and in the same breath request them to keep his plan to divorce her secret from Tiffany.

In fact, Rafiq was starting to think that if the child turned out to be his, he might as well stay married to Tiffany....

Last night had only served to confirm that the nights alone would make it worth the sacrifice.

"I hadn't exactly meant to stay here—in bed—all day," she murmured breathlessly.

He reared over her and the tangled sheets fell away. "Why not?"

Tiffany glanced at his naked chest. When her gaze returned to his, her eyes glittered bright gold. "What will people say if we remain barricaded up in the bed-chamber?"

He shrugged. Who cared? "That we just got married? That I can't keep my hands off my wife?"

He matched actions to the words and ran a hand along the delicate curves of her body. She shuddered and instantly his own desire rocketed.

"Rafiq!"

"What?" He bent forward to taste her again.

She fended him off with flat palms. "We shouldn't..."

"Why not?"

Her palms softened against his shoulders, toying with the sleek muscles of his arms, moving over his shoulders, drawing him close.

"You know," she breathed, "I can't think of a single good reason anymore."

"I am pleased." Rafiq's breath mingled with hers.

Then there were no more words, only touches so sensual, so arousing, that he forgot about everything except the woman in his arms.

The first week after their wedding passed in a whirl.

It was Thursday by the time they finally returned to Katar, the capital. That evening, Tiffany crossed the threshold of the dining salon in Rafiq's home and came to an abrupt halt.

She had not yet called her mother back—or discussed the possibility of a visit with Rafiq. Her poor mother must be going nuts.

"What is it?"

Rafiq moved from where he'd been standing beside the highly polished table. As he came toward her, Tiffany took in the black trousers and loose white shirt he wore. No dark suit. Yet the casual clothes only served to heighten his raw masculinity, and the top button left undone to reveal the smooth skin of his throat underlined it.

Tiffany jerked her attention away from that taunting bit of naked skin and back to his face. "Nothing. I just remembered something I've been meaning to do." She glanced around. "Where's Lily tonight?"

"We're married—there's no longer any need for my aunt to stay with us."

"Oh."

His aunt's presence had been comforting. Without her there was suddenly a whole new tension in the air.

Before she could bolt, Rafiq pulled the high-backed chair out for her.

"Thank you." Conscious of him behind her, Tiffany sat down. He smelled of sandalwood and soap and an exotic spice she didn't recognize. Focusing on the woven table mat in front of her, she gathered her thoughts as Rafiq settled into the seat opposite her. Finally she lifted her head.

Hamal, his chef, had entered and was lighting a dozen candles arranged in a heavy wrought-iron holder on the table. The golden glow of the flame washed over Rafiq's skin, the warmth softening the harsh, handsome features. Tiffany's stomach tightened and desire, never far away, licked at her belly.

As soon as Hamal retreated, Rafiq stretched out and took her hand. "Would you like to meet me for lunch tomorrow? A date? To make up for the lack of them before our wedding?"

She flushed with pleasure. When Rafiq was in this mood, he was downright easy to like. "That would be nice."

He relaxed slightly. "I've booked a table at the best Japanese restaurant in the city."

"Japanese?" she asked, surprised.

He nodded and Tiffany couldn't help noticing how the candlelight moved lovingly across his hair, bringing a bright sheen to the rich sable. As Hamal returned to place large, white plates on the place mats before them, Rafiq released her fingers. Unexpectedly, she found herself missing his touch.

"There's a fairly large Japanese community living in Dhahara—part of the booming motor industry. You'll enjoy the food."

"I look forward to it."

"There are some upcoming events I need to discuss with you."

So, not a date. A meeting. A little of the pleasure at his invitation went out of her. "What kind of events?"

Tilting his head to one side he said, "On Saturday

night there's a banquet in aid of the children's wing at the hospital."

No harm could come from attending that. Her wariness had been misplaced. Yet images from last week's newspaper floated through her mind. Pictures of Rafiq and an adoring, beautiful woman. Lily had said that had been at the opening of the hospital's new wing. This time *she* would be at Rafiq's side.

As his wife.

Something of her fierceness must've shown on her face, because Rafiq said, "I know. I know. I should've asked you before, but it slipped my mind." The smoldering look he gave her made it clear exactly what *had* been on his mind. "I'm the guest of honor, so we can't refuse."

Tiffany pushed away the memory of the other woman and took ruthless advantage of his admission of forgetfulness. "I need to ask you something, too."

"To take you shopping for clothes to wear?"

"No. More important."

The sensual warmth evaporated as his gaze jerked back to her face, intense and penetrating. "What is it?"

She wriggled, and crumpled the white linen napkin she'd just unfolded into a ball. "I spoke to my mother a few days ago."

"Your mother?" A crease appeared between his dark brows. "Did you tell her about the wedding?"

Tiffany nodded.

"And your father? Did you get in contact with him, too?"

This time she shook her head. "I'm not ready to talk with him yet." Then she added in a rush of honesty, "I didn't invite my mother to the wedding because I didn't want her to worry about me."

"You think marrying me would concern her?"

"It was easier to present her with a fait accompli." Tiffany helped herself to what looked like meatballs and spooned a mix of eggplant, tomato and okra on the side.

"That way she could do nothing about it."

"Exactly."

"So what's the problem?" he asked slowly.

"She's worried she's not going to see me as often as she'd like. I told her we'd go visit." From the corner of her eye she saw that Rafiq had started to eat, too. "And she's worried about why I married you. I told her I'm pregnant," she added in a rush.

Tiffany took a flatbread from a basket to give herself something to do. The mundane act of breaking the bread and first dipping the bits into olive oil then dredging them in *dukka,* a fragrant mixture of roasted nuts, toasted sesame and coriander seed, steadied her.

"You're not regretting our marriage already?" Rafiq's expression was somber.

Tiffany swallowed. Was he regretting the marriage? Did he feel trapped? "What makes you think that?"

"Good to know there is no cause for concern," he purred. "Though our lovemaking is so passionate that I would find that hard to believe…even though you keep me far away from your heart."

"I'd have to be a fool to let you into my heart. You're a prince of a wealthy desert kingdom. Eligible, rich, good-looking—"

"Thank you." He set down the knife and held up a hand. "I've heard enough. It is quite clear my attributes don't match up to your list."

Her mind went blank. "What list?"

His mouth kinked, but his dark brown eyes were uncomfortably grave. "For your white knight. Your ordinary prince. You want someone ordinary. A house with a white picket fence. Two-point-four children."

Oh, God. Had she told him all about that? "You remembered!"

He inclined his head. "Everything you've ever told me."

Help. "That's not a list. Not really."

At least, it wasn't the complete list. Above all else she wanted a man who loved her more than anything in the world. A man who would never stray and would be happy with her for all of his life. That man wasn't the distant, restless, easily charmed Rafiq ibn Selim Al Dhahara.

"It's just—"

"Just a way to make sure I know I don't qualify, hmm?" He lifted a brow inviting her to agree. "A way to keep me at a distance?"

Despite her sudden loss of appetite, Tiffany tore off a piece of bread and took a bite, chewed and swallowed.

At her sudden preoccupation, he smiled. But his flat eyes held no amusement; they were cool and watchful.

"It's not you…" Her voice trailed away.

"It's you. I know." He nodded. "But I find it interesting that you're prepared to admit you do not let any man close."

"I'm not admitting anything." Frustration filled Tiffany. "Look, it's nothing like that—you're misunderstanding me." But how to explain the fear that filled her? She didn't dare relax around him—it would be too easy to be charmed. Like all the other women he'd joked found him charming.

There, she'd admitted it. To herself. He charmed her. But she'd cut her tongue out before she let him in on the secret. "Surely you can understand that better than anyone in the world?"

"*I* can?"

She nodded. "You keep women at a distance, too."

He shook his head slowly. "Not to the same extent. I've had three very serious relationships. You were a virgin when we met."

"So you do believe me?" Tiffany couldn't believe her ears.

He shrugged. "You told me you're a virgin…I should give you the benefit of the doubt. It's not like you've made a habit of lying to me."

She wanted his unconditional trust.

He wasn't ready to give it.

Deflated, Tiffany backtracked to what they'd been discussing. "You might have had three serious relationships, but you didn't marry any of those women. Even though I'm prepared to stake money on it that they would've been more suitable for the position of your princess than I could ever be."

His hand closed over hers where it lay, clenched. "None of them matter now. You are my princess. And while you let me close in our marriage bed, there's always a distance between us. And I know why."

"My father has nothing to do with this!" she said quickly.

Didn't Rafiq realize he did exactly the same thing? As passionate as he was in bed, he was remote out of it. She was starting to hate the expressionless mask he wore to close the world—and her—out.

"I think your father has everything to do with it. I'm looking forward to meeting him."

"You're not likely to meet my father—we're not speaking." Determined to put a damper on his enthusiasm, she didn't notice his intense interest. "It's only my mother I intend to visit. She sounded lonely on the phone. And she's worried about our sudden marriage. When can we go?"

Two furrows creased his brow. "Should you be flying in your condition?"

"Pregnant women fly all the time."

"Not my wife."

His possessive growl caused her to blink.

Softening his tone, he added, "Why don't you invite your mother to come visit you here? My schedule is too full to travel right now—and later may be too close to the birth."

Not a no, but not a yes, either.

A twinge of apprehension shot through her. Was he refusing to let her leave? Did he intend to keep her hostage in Dhahara till the baby was born...or longer?

The more she considered that, the more apprehensive she grew.

"If you can't come, then I'll just have to go alone." She pushed her chair back. "Now I'm tired. I'm going to bed."

Alone, Rafiq retreated to the darkened courtyard at the heart of the house. During the day the back wall opened to a wide balcony that overlooked the desert on the edge of the city. But now the courtyard retained the warmth from the hot day in the paving around the pool.

Having shed his clothes, Rafiq sank into the silken water, and fought to clear his head. There was a sense of emptiness within him at Tiffany's departure. The night of pleasure he'd anticipated had been lost. Most frustratingly he couldn't identify how everything had gone so awry in such a short space of time. He'd forced himself not to follow her. She was pregnant. She needed rest. And he had no confidence in his ability to leave her alone.

This time he didn't think making love to her would have eased the tension that had flared between them.

Reaching the far end of the pool, he hoisted himself out and sat on the pool's edge.

Moonlight streaked the water's surface with silver stripes.

Rafiq swung his feet in circles and the silver light broke up as the water rippled, changing the pattern. Like Tiffany. Every time he thought he'd worked her out, Tiffany revealed another facet.

She was far more complex than he would ever have guessed that first night when he'd written her off as a woman after as much money as she could get in the shortest space of time—even if she had to use her body to get it.

He'd been wrong about that.

So wrong…

Feet still in the water, Rafiq propped his elbows on the stone behind him that was still warm from the day's heat and leaned back to stare into the arc of the desert night sky. With the moon so bright, only the most determined stars were visible. One star sparkled brighter than the rest in its group. His gaze homed in on it. It reminded him of his wife—the one who stood out, fascinating him.

In his heart he knew Tiffany had been an innocent— even though his brain was reluctant to accept it. Because that would mean that only he could be her baby's father— that his judgment of her had been criminally wrong.

He was rarely wrong.

And Rafiq was not yet ready to concede that he'd erred in his judgment. Certainly not aloud—as Tiffany had clearly wanted him to do earlier. When the sparkle had gone out of her eyes, he'd wished he had.

Sitting up, he reached for his towel.

Nor did he want to examine too closely why he was

reluctant to admit that he'd been wrong, why it shamed him to have judged her so harshly. He, Rafiq ibn Selim Al Dhahara, who had always been ruled by numbers and logic, had lost his head, and made a spectacular error.

And it all raised another interesting question...

One only Tiffany could answer. Rafiq paused in the act of toweling his hair. If she hadn't slept with him because of money, then why had she done it? Why had she let a stranger take something so precious?

She accused him of keeping women at a distance, of being the last man she'd ever wanted to marry. So why sleep with him when there'd been little hope of seeing him again?

She wanted an ordinary man, a house with a white picket fence, and a pigeon pair. That's what she'd harked back to every time—a fairy tale. He threw the towel to one side. They both knew he was as far from her ordinary prince as it was possible to get.

Water churned angrily as he pulled his legs out of the pool and rose to his full height.

The only answer that made any kind of convoluted sense gave him no comfort at all. Tiffany had gone for a man so far removed from everything she said she wanted because deep in her heart she had no intention of loving anyone. Ever. Not even the ordinary man he'd been so knotted up inside about.

She'd let him close only because he could never be her dream man.

He had to live with that. Or make her accept him as he was, royal prince, international banker, father of her child.

And most importantly, her husband.

Eleven

The Japanese restaurant Rafiq ushered Tiffany into the next day was decorated with deceptive simplicity. Low ceilings and white papered screens set in black lacquered frames gave the space intimacy, while gold-trimmed red wall banners and bamboo shoots in large ceramic pots emblazoned with gold pagodas added touches of luxury.

Rafiq was warmly welcomed by the elderly couple who owned the restaurant, whom he introduced to Tiffany as Mei and Taeko Nakamura.

To the Nakamuras he declared, "I have brought my wife to meet you."

Taeko bowed politely in her direction yet Tiffany suspected it was Mei's black-currant eyes that missed little.

"You said nothing of a wife when we saw you two weeks ago. I suppose this is the reason why you canceled your lunch last week. But shouldn't we at least have read about your wedding in the papers?"

"It will be announced in tomorrow's paper," Rafiq promised, grinning down at the little woman, not looking the least bit chastened.

That was more than Tiffany knew. She opened her mouth to interrupt him, but Mei was already saying, "So we know a secret." And her contemplative eyes settled on Tiffany's midline. Yet, much to Tiffany's relief, she didn't ask the obvious question and led them instead to a table in a corner secluded by screens.

What surprised Tiffany was the way Rafiq's austere features had lit up with pleasure at the sight of the elderly couple, making him appear quite different from the man who only ever presented an emotionless facade.

Nor did he need to order.

Taeko brought a platter of sashimi tuna and pink salmon, and it was quickly apparent that Rafiq was a frequent visitor, though Taeko produced a menu for Tiffany's inspection.

Mei dug out a cell phone and passed it to Rafiq to admire the latest photos of her granddaughter. He made appropriate noises and asked questions about the child whose name appeared to be Keiko, revealing an intimate familiarity with the family. Tiffany couldn't prevent a pang of sadness. If only he'd shown some of this easy joy when she'd shown him the scan images of their baby...

Instead he'd been horrified by the possibility that she might actually be pregnant with his child.

"The tuna is flown in daily," Rafiq told her as Taeko brought the beef teriyaki she'd ordered. "I never eat anything else here."

"I'll stick to beef—rather than raw fish," she said lightly, not wanting to make a point about her pregnancy.

"Delicious," she declared after the first mouthful of her meal.

As she tucked in, she couldn't help wondering whether Rafiq would one day show the same interest in their child as he'd shown for Keiko.

How would she feel about that interest? Rafiq appeared reluctant for her to leave the country to visit her mother. If he grew invested in their daughter, it was possible that he would take over the decision making for her child and leave her with no say.

It was something Tiffany had not considered in any depth before.

Foolish, perhaps.

Given his opinion about her in the past, she'd never anticipated that Rafiq would want to marry her. When he'd proposed, it had been so clear that his major preoccupation was waiting for the baby to be born so that he could wiggle off the hook of paternal responsibility. She'd never contemplated that he might actually want their daughter... or be eager for input into her upbringing.

Tiffany bit her lip.

She'd wanted her daughter to one day have the right to know her father. She'd been prepared to allow some kind of visitation schedule. But she'd never intended to put her daughter within Rafiq's total control.

Breathing deeply to control her rising panic, she tried to focus on what Mei was saying to Rafiq.

"How are Shafir and Megan? You have not brought them for a while."

"They spend every spare moment at Qasr Al-Ward." Rafiq rolled his eyes to the ceiling. "The price of love."

Relief seeped through Tiffany as she watched him joking with the Nakamuras.

Rafiq was no threat to her...or her daughter. He wasn't

a monster. He was only a man. A busy man, a banker of international repute. A desert prince. With a family who were loving.

Why would he want to take over the life of the daughter he'd disputed was his? Even when the tests proved he was the father, it was unlikely that he'd have the time—or the interest—to be a hands-on father.

As the reality of the situation sank in, she started to relax.

Taeko gave a sharp bark of laughter at something Rafiq said. He replied in Japanese, his eyes crinkling, and Mei swatted his arm with the white linen napkin she held.

Rafiq was laughing, his ebony eyes gleaming with mirth.

"You speak Japanese," Tiffany blurted out.

"He speaks German and a bit of Spanish, too." Mei gave her an odd look, and Tiffany felt herself coloring. What kind of wife lacked such basic knowledge about her husband?

She'd been so caught up in her own situation, her pregnancy, her parents' problems, their hasty marriage, she'd barely bothered to learn much about her new husband.

He smiled across the table at her, and her heart leaped at the understanding in his eyes. "What languages do you speak, Tiffany?"

"English and French."

Mei glanced at him in astonishment. "You don't know? Rafiq! What have you two been talking about?"

"Important things!" Rafiq's eyes held a wicked gleam, and Taeko roared with laughter.

Tiffany's flush deepened. Rafiq knew she spoke French. He'd covered up for her. She could've kissed him for making it clear that she wasn't the only one who had been neglectful.

"We will leave the two of you alone to learn more important things about each other." Mei took her husband by the arm and steered him away.

Once the incorrigible pair had departed, Tiffany asked, "How did you meet them?"

"They came to the bank one day needing a loan against the business." His eyes grew somber.

His expression sent a chill down Tiffany's spine. She waited, knowing there must be more to the story.

"Mei had grown so upset that security had to be called to calm her. I heard the commotion, and went to see what it was about. After all, I am ultimately responsible for the safety of everyone in the building."

"What was she upset about?"

"Their granddaughter needed a bone-marrow transplant. It was a procedure that was not available in Dhahara at the time. They needed to go to America. The business was already heavily in debt because of Keiko's medical bills."

"You helped them."

"I never said that."

He didn't need to. Tiffany studied him. "That was very generous of you."

"It wasn't only me—others helped, too. Children like Keiko are the reason I'm so involved in fundraising for the hospital." He glanced away from her intense gaze. "After lunch I am taking you shopping."

"Shopping?" The sudden transition to something so inconsequential confused her. "For Keiko?"

"No, for the press conference in the morning where our marriage will be formally announced and for tomorrow night's banquet. We agreed you needed clothes. You'll need something suitable to wear."

"Press conference?" The thought of the all-too-familiar paparazzi flashlights that dogged her parents' every step filled her with horror. "Can't we just release a statement?"

He shook his head. "This is part of my duty to the people of my country."

Just thinking about a press conference made her stomach sink. Thankfully, she hadn't been photographed for years—her parents had protected her from the relentless glare of Hollywood publicity. And living in Auckland had helped. Now that anonymity would prove a blessing. It was highly unlikely that the press would connect Tiffany, née Smith, wife of Sheikh Rafiq ibn Selim Al Dhahara, with Tiffany Smith, daughter of notorious film director Taylor Smith.

But Rafiq was newsworthy.

And Tiffany knew what would happen *if* her father glimpsed the photos. He would swoop, and try and take over running her life. She already had enough doubts about her own ability to run it, so she certainly didn't need her father wading into the fray.

Laying trembling fingers on his, she murmured, "Rafiq, what if the press report who my father is?"

He closed his free hand over the top of hers. "You need to reconcile with your father. Wait—" he said when she would've interrupted him. "Not for his sake but for your own peace of mind."

Tiffany stared at him rebelliously. "That's all very well, but what do we do if anyone asks today?"

He patted her hand. "Don't worry about it, I'll take care of everything. You worry about looking like a princess. Now let's go buy clothes."

Tiffany fought the urge to tell him she didn't need any clothes. Swiftly she reviewed the contents of her luggage. The long, slim gray skirt and white shirt she'd worn the day she'd arrived would not be glamorous enough for the media baying for photos of the royal sheikh's new bride. Her classic black trousers were not feminine enough and neither of the two maxi dresses she'd packed would be formal enough. And the white dress she'd worn the day she'd met his family was far too unsophisticated for the banquet in the evening—even if it had been created by a young designer whose dresses she loved. And the long dress with gold embroidery that Rafiq had produced for the wedding was far too elaborate for a morning press conference.

It galled her to admit Rafiq was one hundred percent right. None of the clothes she'd brought with her could be described as suitable.

Finally she said, "Okay, let's go shopping."

A discreet bronze wall plaque identified the high-end fashion house Rafiq took her to as Madame Fleur's. It would not have been out of place on Rodeo Drive. The interior of beech-and-chrome cabinetry with glass shelves and black marble floor tiles gave it a sophisticated edge. The black-and-silver labels on the meager range of garments on the racks held no prices. But the cut and quality of the clothes assured Tiffany the cost would be exorbitant.

Far more than she could afford to be indebted to Rafiq at present.

"Rafiq, I don't think—"

"Don't think. Madame and I will take care of everything, won't we?" From where he'd sunk onto a black velvet couch, Rafiq cast the charming smile that Tiffany was starting to recognize at the elegant middle-aged woman whose straight black skirt and black flounced shirt shrieked "French fashion." Predictably, Madame almost swooned and hurriedly agreed.

Tiffany's mouth tightened.

"I can choose my own clothes." It annoyed her that he thought she had no taste, no sense of style.

Swooping on a rack of satin and silks, she selected a dress that wasn't quite the shade of gold or honey or amber, but a mix of all three. At the sight of the cut, she hesitated. Only a woman with supreme self-confidence would wear a dress like this.

"I was thinking of something darker, more formal," Rafiq said, rising from his position on the couch. He picked a wooden hanger off a rack and held up a black satin dress with layered flounces from the hip down. "This is perfect."

"The black dress is beautiful, so elegant," Madame said after a rapid, assessing glance at Rafiq's face.

And very expensive.

Madame was determined to make a sale.

Tiffany suppressed a growl. Did everyone do exactly as he wanted?

"This one." Stubbornly Tiffany pointed to the dress she'd picked, her momentary hesitation forgotten.

"I don't think—" Rafiq paused. Passing the black dress into Madame's waiting arms, he smiled and came toward her with long, pantherish strides. Putting his hands on her shoulders he gazed down into her eyes, his own filled with velvety admiration. "You will look beautiful in whatever you wear. I want people to see you as I do and black suits you."

"Okay, I'll try it first," she found herself saying. A hint of spine had her adding, "But I do prefer the other dress."

He brushed his lips against her forehead. "Thank you for trying on the black."

* * *

Rafiq knew he'd made the right choice. The dress Tiffany had chosen would be too garish. Black was sedate. Black befitted the wife of a prince of Dhahara.

When the curtains parted, she reappeared looking exactly as he'd expected. Elegant. Untouchable. *Suitable*.

"Excellent." He turned to Madame. "We'll take it."

Tiffany's expression grew rebellious. "Hang on. I don't often wear black."

He approached her and stroked her cheek. Lowering his voice so only she could hear, he murmured, "You were wearing black the night I met you."

She shuddered. "And what a mistake that was."

He couldn't deny that the cheap, shiny fabric of the too-tight dress with its short skirt and tight layers had been a little tacky. But she hadn't had the benefit of his—and Madame's—discerning taste. Although he had to admit that since that night Tiffany had worn surprisingly conservative clothes.

"That was Renate's dress—not mine." She spun away, and his fingers fell to his side. "Now I'll try the other dress."

Inside the dressing-room cubicle Tiffany found that she was trembling. Not with fear but frustration…and rising fury. She put her hands over her face. How could she have chickened out like that? Why hadn't she told Rafiq she wanted to select her own dress, something *she* liked? If he wanted to choose her clothes, he should wear them!

She gave a snort of angry laughter.

All her life she'd let people run her life—make choices and decisions for her. Her father. Her teachers. Imogen. Renate.

It wasn't happening anymore.

Her hands fell away from her face, and she stared at her image in the mirror with new eyes. She was pregnant. Soon she'd be a mother. She was in charge of her own life…and her daughter's. For a couple of minutes out there she'd wimped out when she'd agreed to try on the dress Rafiq had picked—and now he thought he'd won.

He almost had.

Yanking the zipper down, she slid the black dress over her hips and stepped out of it, then hung it on a padded wooden hanger.

The cubicle door opened and Madame swayed in, holding the dress that had caused all the trouble.

"Thank you." Tiffany gave the designer a demure smile as she took the dress. Her most charming smile—she could take a leaf out of Rafiq's book. She had no intention of allowing Rafiq to step in and take over—even if he was her husband. He might be rich. He might be a sheikh. He might be a royal prince. But she wasn't going to let him strip her of the independence and self-respect she'd managed to salvage in the past few months. If she did, she might as well go back home. And tell her father that he had won: she'd come home pregnant, penniless and needing someone else to take charge of her future.

This was no longer about a dress—whatever the darned color.

It was about her…her baby…and *their* future.

Rafiq had no faith in her taste. Based on Renate's dress, she couldn't really blame him. But none of the clothes he'd seen her in since had remotely resembled that awful outfit.

As the dress slithered over her head, Tiffany hoped wildly she had not miscalculated. Too late. She couldn't fold and let Rafiq choose what she was going to wear for the rest of their lives; she had to show him that unlike all the other women he knew, he couldn't simply get what he wanted from her with a charming smile or a fake caress.

Behind her Madame eased the zipper up. Tiffany heard her gasp.

"Très magnifique."

Tiffany spun around. The mirror showed a different woman to the black-clad one who had stood in front of it only minutes ago. This woman was young and vibrant…with a touch of vulnerability and an understated earthiness.

The dress was perfect.

It was her.

For one wild moment uncertainty engulfed her. Could she let Rafiq see her like this? The whole world? She hesitated. Then her spine firmed.

She wasn't ashamed of who she was.

Before she could have any further misgivings, she pushed the cubicle door open, and stepped proudly out, her head held high.

At the sight of her, Rafiq's first reaction was a blast of pure, primal possessive desire. Tiffany was his. All his. No man was going to wrest her from him. Ordinary or otherwise. His second thought was that the color could've been created especially for her. It was hard to see where skin ended and dress began—she'd struck lucky with her impulsive choice.

Instead of looking gaudy, the shade gave her skin a honey tone and turned her hair the burnished shade of bronze.

"What do you think?" Her eyes challenged his.

He gulped.

He didn't dare tell her what he was thinking.

That way lay…

Insanity.

Trying for cool, he said, "It suits you." But he ruined the effect by glancing down at the curves that the dress hugged. Rafiq started to sweat.

"Better than the black?" At the note in her voice his gaze jerked up.

She was taunting him.

No woman dared to taunt him.

Ever.

Even if she was his wife.

His eyes narrowed to slits. This time he took his time looking her over. When he finally reached her face, her lips were parted. He knew she'd be breathing in little gasps. Against his will, his body started to harden.

"Definitely better than the black." His voice came out in a hoarse croak. Without looking away he said to Madame, "We will take this dress."

Then he smiled slowly at Tiffany. No point wasting more time arguing over clothes, not when he was in such a hurry to get home and strip his wife of every item she was wearing.

So he said softly, "Now, which outfit did you have in mind for the press conference?"

Twelve

The front door of Rafiq's home clicked shut behind them.

"Come here, wife."

At Rafiq's growl, Tiffany glanced over her shoulder… and clashed with his hot gaze. He'd barely spoken in the Mercedes-Benz on the way home. And now he expected her to fall into his arms?

"Wait a moment—"

Before she could finish, he closed in on her. Despite her intention of resisting him, desire sparked into an inferno as his lips claimed hers. His hands gripped her shoulders. She swayed back until she came up against the coolness of the plastered wall. Rafiq's body was hard and solid against her curves, and his hands softened to caress the crest of her shoulders, then moved in tantalizing circles under the weight of her hair.

He kissed her until she could barely think.

To her astonishment Tiffany felt unaccountably safe

crushed against him. When he raised his head, it sank in that they were indulging in a passionate embrace, in broad daylight, in the lobby of his home with guards on the other side of the door and his staff in the house.

The impropriety of it made her flush. Pulling back from him, from the intensity of his touch, she yanked the neckline of her dress back into place. "Rafiq, what are you thinking? Your staff could walk in on us at any moment."

"I called and dismissed the house staff. And I secured the locks on the front door and set the security system when we came in." Smug satisfaction glowed good-humoredly in his eyes. "No one is going to interrupt us."

"You planned this!" she accused.

"No, it was a spontaneous reaction to the show you put on at Madame Fleur's store."

That damned dress was still causing trouble!

Before she could put the blame where it rightly belonged, he placed the tip of his index finger against her lips. "Enough talking, I want to kiss you."

Unable to resist a wicked temptation, Tiffany slid her tongue across the pad of his fingertip. He tasted of male and the tang of salt. She licked again. Slowly. Deliberately.

This time he took her mouth with a harsh groan.

The hunger rose more swiftly this time. His lips played with hers until Tiffany gave him a gentle nip. "Kiss me properly."

She hooked her hands behind his nape and pulled his mouth down square on hers. Her hunger silenced the wisecracks, she noted with satisfaction.

The next second the world spun around her. The floor tilted and the dark blue of the walls filled her vision. Tiffany clutched at the front of his shirt. "What are you doing?"

"Taking you somewhere where we can pursue this further." His lips hovered near her ear, the soft whisper of his breath sending delicious tremors though her. "Have you ever made love in a pool?"

"You know I haven't." Excitement quaked through her. "Have you?"

"Never."

"Then we'll have to teach each other how it's done."

They made it to the edge of the pool.

Rafiq deposited her on a lounging chair before straightening and wrenching off his tie. His shirt and trousers followed, landing in a heap on the mosaic tiles. In seconds he stood naked before her.

Breathing quickly, Tiffany eyed her husband with open admiration.

Muscled shoulders sloped to a lean waist, and his stomach was flat and taut. Her fingers itched to stroke the sleek skin.

He dropped down on his knees beside her, and he touched the length of her leg where the filmy maxi dress had fallen away with reverence. "Your skin is so soft," he whispered, "I can never have enough of you."

One day he would—it was how he was made, she knew. But that day wasn't here yet.

For now, he was all hers.

And she wasn't going to let him forget it.

He kissed the inside of her thighs, his fingers slipping under the lacy edge of her panties. Tiffany's breath caught as he slid the scraps of lace down her legs. She shifted restlessly. He was touching her again, making her sigh with delight, his fingers slick against her, arousing her to fever pitch.

She threw her head back and squeezed her eyes shut,

concentrating on the sensations that he aroused. The pleasure twisted higher...tighter.

"More," she moaned, her fingers reaching for him.

Her hand found his hardness, closed around him, felt him jerk.

Then he was on the lounger beside her, pulling her up against him, spoon-fashion, curled behind her. He drew her closer, hesitated, then surged inside her.

She gasped.

He started to move, slowly at first, then quicker. His mouth closed on her neck, nipping gently, causing her to shudder at the sensitive sensation. For a moment she hung suspended in space, a place between, where she was neither herself nor his, but something between. Then she shuddered and whirled into a world of pure pleasure.

When she'd finally come back to earth, she turned to face him, and hooked her arms around his neck. Staring deeply into his eyes, she whispered, "Oh, please say we can do that again?"

Yet the next morning nothing of the playful lover of the previous night remained.

Rafiq was all business.

Tiffany wore the apricot-colored suit she'd picked out that did amazing things for her skin. She knew she looked her best.

Rafiq had barely glanced at her. All he was intent on was lecturing her. If she hadn't known better, she might have thought he was nervous.

"Nothing will be said about how we met," he reminded her as the cavalcade that they were part of turned into the road in front of the palace, the king's main residence in Katar. "Do not get drawn into the work you were doing.

As far as the public is concerned we met through a mutual university friend."

When the doors of the limousine opened, she was ready for the popping clicks of the camera. Putting on her most gracious smile, she allowed Rafiq to help her out.

The press conference started innocuously enough—with Rafiq in total command.

The announcement of their marriage was made, causing a buzz of excitement. Rafiq indulged the journalists, fielding questions, posing with Tiffany for shots, until one journalist called to Rafiq to kiss her.

Her heart thudding, Tiffany turned, raising her face to his. One arm came around her shoulders, the other around her waist and then he paused, staring down at her.

A long moment passed, then all the clicks of cameras and flashing of lights faded. It was a taut moment, full of unspoken tension.

Tiffany waited, face uplifted for the kiss that never came.

Finally, amidst her confusion, he let her go, with a hoarse mutter in Arabic that she did not understand.

Then he took her by the hand and dragged her out of the auditorium, the gaggle of royal aides scurrying in their wake.

Tiffany hurried alongside Rafiq as he strode outside, his fingers tightly holding hers. One glance at his face revealed this was not a good time to ask what she desperately wanted to know.

What had gone wrong?

* * *

That mysterious moment this morning had wired Rafiq. Every time he looked at Tiffany, brushed her hand, a current of electricity blasted him.

Lust, he told himself as he strode the bank's hallways.

Triggered by that damned dress yesterday…and the cataclysmic passion that had followed.

He'd never intended to kiss Tiffany in front of the media this morning—his conservative father would never tolerate such a display. Yet by Allah he'd been tempted…

He'd almost done it.

It shocked him, how near he'd come to the edge.

Where was his control? His common sense?

His hunger, regardless of the cameras, had stunned him. Never before had his private emotions threatened to spill over into a public place.

Still brooding, he turned at the tap on his shoulder. He greeted his eldest brother.

"You are not with your wife," said Khalid.

"I left her in Aunt Lily's hands—gave her a chance to meet other women here tonight."

"Father wants to run a background check on her. He says we know nothing about her—he's worried you rushed into this marriage too impulsively."

"And Shafir didn't?"

"Ah, but that was different. Father was making sure Megan was being kept under surveillance, remember?"

Rafiq couldn't stop the jab of irritation. "It's a little late for that. I know everything I need to know about my wife. We announced our marriage to the world this morning. What does Father hope to achieve?"

Khalid gave him a wry grin. "Your happiness, probably.

I will tell him to forget the idea. He should be thankful that you are married—it's what he wanted after all."

"You will be next," warned Rafiq, his good humor restored.

Aunt Lily had introduced Tiffany to a circle of women as Rafiq's new wife, and Tiffany was aware of their curiosity. She'd warded off the more nosy questions with good grace, and cautiously answered the innocuous ones.

"Your dress…is it from Madame Fleur's?" asked one woman, openly admiring it.

Tiffany smiled demurely. Though a silk wrap was draped around her shoulders, she knew even without it the dress would be perfectly respectable. It was the cut and color that made it look so revealing, not the flesh it exposed. "Yes, it is."

"Not Rafiq's usual taste," said a beautiful woman who had joined the huddle. She was clad in a floor-length black sheath similar to the dress Rafiq had wanted Tiffany to wear tonight. "My name is Shenilla."

Tiffany smiled again. "Nice to meet you, Shenilla." Aware that everyone had fallen silent, she said, "Your dress is lovely."

Shenilla smoothed her hands over her hips, the movement oddly sinuous. "Rafiq chose it for me while we were still…together."

This time the lack of enthusiasm in the slanting eyes was overt.

Uh-oh. The woman in the newspaper photo. The daughter of the wealthy benefactor. And obviously one of Rafiq's former loves. "Oh."

Two of the group hurriedly excused themselves. Tiffany said something meaningless to the woman on the other side of Shenilla—then discovered it was Dr. Farouk, the doctor she and Rafiq had visited about DNA testing. A quick glance showed no sign of Rafiq.

Thrown to the lions—or in this case the lioness.

The image brought no amusement.

A waiter appeared and murmured something in the doctor's ear.

Dr. Farouk gave Tiffany an apologetic look. "Excuse me, duty calls—one of the older women is feeling breathless. I must check on her."

Left alone with Shenilla, Tiffany considered her next move.

She had to admit to a certain curiosity. This must surely be one of the women whom Rafiq had loved—then fallen out of love with. The woman was incredibly beautiful, with a regal elegance that made it obvious why Rafiq had picked her. Of course her father's wealth would've made her a good match, too. Tiffany was instantly conscious of the differences between them. This woman's hair was restrained in a smooth knot, her slanting eyes heavily outlined with kohl.

"Rafiq grows tired of all his women."

Tiffany started to object to being referred to as one of Rafiq's women, to point out she was his wife, but the sheen of moisture coating Shenilla's eyes stopped her.

"I was so certain I would be the one he married. Two years of my life I gave him, hoping every day that he would ask me to be his wife. Instead, not long before he went off to negotiate that hotel deal in Hong Kong, he invited me and my parents out to dinner and told us that our relationship was over." Shenilla swiped her fingertips under her bottom lashes. "I'm sorry, I must be embarrassing you."

Sympathy swept Tiffany, along with another sharp, piercing unidentified emotion. Rafiq had told her that it was the pressure from his family, from the woman and her family, that drove him to break off his relationships. Shenilla had just confirmed it.

"Not at all." She touched the other woman's arm. "You will find someone."

Shenilla sniffed, then nodded. "You are kind. I hope you will not suffer the same hurt, too."

Tiffany wanted to reassure her, tell her she'd been immunized against love a long time ago…but a painful tightness in the vicinity of her heart stopped her. Rafiq was nothing like her father.

"The only comfort I can offer you is that Rafiq is reputed to be faithful while the relationship lasts. A code with him. But there is always the knowledge that one day it will end." Shenilla gave a watery smile. "Although it must be different for you, as he loved you enough to marry you."

Before Tiffany could blurt out that he didn't love her, a hand settled on her waist.

"I see you have met Shenilla." There was a dangerous note in her husband's liquid voice.

Tiffany slid him a sideways glance, and caught the edge in his examination of his former lover.

"We're admiring each other's dresses." Then she remembered Rafiq had picked out the other woman's dress, and added hurriedly, "And comparing style notes. Shenilla was saying that black is one of her favorite colors."

Shenilla shot her a grateful look.

Rafiq pulled her closer to his side. Tiffany suppressed the fierce urge to move away. Couldn't he see the pain he was causing Shenilla? Was he so insensitive? No, he wasn't obtuse. He was doing it deliberately, warning the other woman that he would stand no threat to Tiffany.

She didn't know whether to hug him or scold him for his protectiveness. For the sake of Shenilla's pride, she decided to pretend she hadn't noticed, and continued chatting about the latest fall fashions, while Rafiq vibrated with tension beside her.

A mix of emotions rattled her. She wanted to shake him. She wanted to kiss him. What on earth was wrong with her?

He tilted his head sideways, and gave her a smile. Her heart rolled over.

Oh, no. Please. Anything but that.

Falling for Rafiq was the dumbest thing she could do. Already he'd been pressured by circumstance—and by a need to legitimize their child—to marry her. She'd unwittingly caught him in exactly the kind of trap that he'd avoided so assiduously all his life.

How could he feel anything but resentment toward her?

Thirteen

The intrusive ring of her cell phone woke Tiffany several mornings later.

Rolling over, she groped with one hand for the bedside table, and the ringing stopped.

With a groan she sat up. The first thing she realized was that the morning roller-coaster ride that her stomach had been on for weeks seemed to be over. The second was that the sound of running water meant Rafiq was in the shower in the adjoining bathroom. He hadn't yet gone to work. Checking the missed call, Tiffany recognized her mother's cell phone number. She hit Redial.

What could be wrong?

"Darling, where are you staying?" Her mother's voice sounded surprisingly clear.

Tiffany tried to collect her thoughts. "What do you mean?"

"We're here. In Dhahara."

"We?"

"Your father and I."

Tiffany stomach bottomed out, and she squeezed her eyes shut in horror.

"Where?"

"At the airport. We're about to catch a cab to come and see you."

No!

She heard the glass door click as Rafiq opened it. Any moment he'd be back in the bedroom. He knew she missed her mother; he'd said she needed to reconcile with her father. Had he arranged this?

"Mom—"

"There were photos of you all over the front page of the national newspaper that we were given in the airplane. But we couldn't understand a word of the story."

Darn it.

"Why is Dad with you?"

"Tiffany, I had to tell him about your marriage—I couldn't keep it from him. He's worried about you, darling. So we decided to come and see how you were."

Not worried so much as wanting to make sure she took his advice. Tiffany sighed.

"I wish you'd let me know you were going to tell him." She would've preferred to tell him herself.

"Your new husband is a hunk." Her mother sounded downright coy as she sidestepped Tiffany's comment. "You never mentioned that."

Straining her ears for sounds of the "hunk," Tiffany ignored the subtle rebuke. "Mom, why don't you go and book in at one of the city's hotels? I'll come see you in a couple of hours. Then maybe we can arrange to spend a couple of days together. Maybe we can go on an excursion into the desert."

"But we want to see you—"

The sound of footsteps made her say hurriedly, "I've got to go—I'll call you later."

Rafiq stood in the arch that separated the bedroom from the bathroom. "Who are you going to call later?" he asked, raising a dark eyebrow.

She hesitated. "My mom. Rafiq…"

He came swiftly across the room. "Problems?"

The concern in his eyes made her feel simply awful.

"Not really. Rafiq—" she bit her lip "—my mother is here, in Dhahara."

His expression brightened. "That's good. You wanted to visit your mother, now she can set her mind at rest."

She had to ask. "Did you call my mom and set this up?"

"No!" His brows jerked together. "I don't even have her contact details, come to think of it."

He had all the resources he needed to have found her if he'd wanted to. But she couldn't doubt him. She had to trust him at his word.

"Sorry." She chewed her lip again: "My father is here, too. I asked Mom why he came, and she says he's worried about me."

"Sounds like a father. Invite them to dinner." Rafiq walked into the closet. When he came out he was wearing trousers and shrugging on a business shirt. "They can stay here—there are plenty of bedchambers."

Oh, God. "You don't understand. My father always expects me to do what he wants."

He paused in the act of buttoning his shirt and raised that expressive eyebrow. "You're a married woman now."

"In his eyes I'll always be his little girl who can't run her own life."

"You're a grown woman. You're married, and soon you'll be having a baby. You'll be a parent yourself. He can only run your life if you let him."

"You're so right," she said in wonder. She'd never thought of herself in the context of being a mother in quite that way before—or how it affected her in relation to her father.

"You don't need to love him any less—he'll always be your father."

There was something so liberating in his words. She'd fought with her father so much over her freedom that they'd isolated each other. It didn't need to be that way. She would make her own choices, make it clear to her father this was her life, her choice, but that she would always love him.

If there was no battle, there could be no hostility. And her father had made his choices, too. He'd chosen Imogen over her mother. She needed to accept that. Her mother had already taken steps to deal with that reality. Now she had to do the same.

Maybe she could salvage something of their father-daughter relationship.

"Thank you, Rafiq." She raised her face to him and accepted his kiss.

"I must go, before you tempt me to collapse beside you and spend the day in bed."

"But, Rafiq "

"Later." He picked up a dark suit jacket and slung it over his shoulder. As he reached the bedroom door he gave her a gentle smile. "Tell your parents I am looking forward to welcoming them to our home."

It was in that moment that Tiffany realized how much she truly loved him.

* * *

Several hours later Rafiq hurried toward the grand salon in his father's palace. He nodded to the aides. The double doors were flung open. Rafiq strode forward.

"Who was it you wanted to meet—"

The king was not alone. Rafiq stopped as he recognized the man seated in the brown leather armchair across from his father.

Sir Julian Carling rose to his feet and stretched out his hand. Rafiq shook it and raised an eyebrow in the king's direction.

"What is this about?"

His father looked wearier than Rafiq had ever seen.

"My son—" He broke off.

"What is it?"

But Rafiq had a sinking feeling that he knew. He gave the hotelier a narrow-eyed glare. Sir Julian looked away first.

"I have been concerned about this woman you have married."

"We have already discussed this, Father."

"I fear that I was too hasty—I should have pursued my first instinct and had her investigated."

"Father—"

The king held up a hand. "Stop. You will listen to what Sir Julian has told me. It is scandalous."

Blood roared in Rafiq's ears as he paced the length of the room. "I am not interested in what Sir Julian has to say about my wife."

The king shook his head sadly. "I fear she will not be your wife for much longer—you will have no choice but to divorce her."

Rafiq spun around. Sir Julian must have seen the rage

in his eyes because the millionaire almost overturned his chair in his haste to stand.

"Now look here, Rafiq—"

"Rafiq!" The lash of the king's tongue called him to order.

He drew a deep, shuddering breath.

"My son, you really do need to hear what Sir Julian is going to say."

"I know what he is going to say."

The king looked shocked. "You knew this woman is a prostitute?"

"That is a lie!"

This time Julian backed away five paces.

It was the king's turn to glance uncertainly at Sir Julian. "You are sure of these facts?"

"She has hoodwinked him," Sir Julian sputtered. "He found her in a flesh club in Hong Kong."

"What do you hope to get out of this?" Rafiq demanded, advancing on the hotelier.

"Your father has agreed that my daughter will make you a perfect wife. But Elizabeth will never agree to marrying a man who already has a wife. You will need to have your marriage annulled—fraud will be reason enough."

Rafiq's anger before was nothing to the rage that consumed him now.

"I do not want your daughter—I already have a wife. And no fraud has been committed that could merit annulling the marriage."

"She lied to you."

Rafiq shook his head. "Not so."

"But Elizabeth is coming to Dhahara to meet you."

"It is a waste of her time—and mine. Nor does it have anything to do with my wife."

"I invited her—" the King broke in "—Sir Julian and I have been talking."

Rafiq knew that tone of old. "What have you been negotiating?"

His father looked guilty. "You have always been a good, loyal son—"

"Oh, no!" Reminding him of his duty would not work this time. Rafiq shook his head.

"Your wife needs to be carefully chosen—"

"I know that—I've already done so."

"Ay, me. This is about sex."

Rafiq stared at his father. "It is not about sex—at least not in the way you mean. My wife is no Mata Hari, she hasn't the loose morals Julian suggests—" in fact the shoe was well and truly on the other foot "—but I admit I cannot keep my hands off her."

The admission freed something within him. Tiffany was important to him, more important than any woman he'd ever known. He wasn't letting her go. She was his.

"This concerns me. You are in the thrall of a woman who is manipulating you. I want you to divorce her before she causes a scandal we cannot fix." The king's face could've been carved from marble.

"Why? So I can marry Elizabeth Carling?"

King Selim's eyes grew shifty. "Sir Julian has offered to make a generous marriage settlement—"

"No! I am not divorcing Tiffany. Nor am I taking another wife. My wife was a virgin the first time I took her to my bed."

The astonishment on his father's face made Rafiq curl his hands into fists at his sides.

"The information I am revealing should be sacred to my wife and me, not dragged out in such a sordid situation."

"My son, if anything happens to me, to your brothers, you will sit on the throne."

The pressure was on. His father was pulling out the big guns. "And why should I marry a woman whose father has no idea of what it means to be faithful?" He didn't even spare Sir Julian a glance. "It was not I who broke marriage vows and slept with a backstreet whore that night in Hong Kong."

Sir Julian turned puce. "You can't talk to—"

"Oh, yes, I can," Rafiq cut in. "I don't want a wife who may have slept with a thousand men because of the example that has been set by her father." He could hear the pulse thudding in his head. "My heirs will be mine alone."

Then he realized what he had said. And the irony of it hit him full force. Tiffany never stopped worrying about the impact her father's notorious affairs would have on his family. He didn't care a fig for that. Yet, even more ironic was the fact that Tiffany was pregnant—and he'd disputed her baby's paternity. And now, in the heat of the accusations, he had defended her.

Because in his heart he knew she had been true. Everything about her was pure.

Her baby was his. He no longer required a DNA test to confirm the fact.

"My wife is pregnant."

A stunned silence followed his announcement. A flash of joy lit up his father's face. "Pregnant? My first grandchild! How I wish your mother was here." Shadows replaced the joy, and King Selim glanced surreptitiously at Sir Julian.

That look told Rafiq what he had feared—that the two of them had already gone far down the road of planning his wedding to Elizabeth Carling—and if Elizabeth hadn't objected to being the second wife, both men would no doubt have let Elizabeth occupy that place.

But Rafiq only wanted one wife, and he had chosen Tiffany.

Part of his choice had embraced a decision to believe in her—there was no reason not to. His place was not here arguing with Sir Julian. His first loyalty lay with his wife—she, and their unborn baby, were now his family.

Fourteen

Tiffany wished Rafiq would come home.

She'd put a call in to his office that her parents were already here. No doubt he would expect her to make the first move to reconcile with her father.

Yet, sitting on the balcony that overlooked a stretch of desert, her father was not making it any easier.

"If you'd stayed home, Tiffany, this mess would never have happened."

Tiffany suppressed the urge to roll her eyes and point out that he was the one who had walked out.

"Taylor, Tiffany is looking forward to having the baby." The stress around her mother's eyes as she ran interference caused Tiffany to wince.

At her father's look of disbelief she only said, "I am, actually."

"This is what you want?" Her father shook his head. "To

be stuck out here on the edge of the desert, where you don't even speak the language, with a man you barely know?"

"The desert is beautiful! Look at all the colors of the setting sun. I can learn the language—and I know enough about Rafiq to know that he's a decent man."

"Decent? What does that mean?"

Anger sparked. She remembered Rafiq's distaste that first night in Le Club when Sir Julian had pulled Renate onto his lap. She thought about how Shenilla had said he only ever dated one woman at a time. "That he would never betray me by running around with other women."

Her father's face changed.

"Oh, come look at this, Taylor, isn't it interesting?"

Her father allowed himself to be distracted by her mother's peacemaking attempts and Tiffany drew an unsteady breath as they both disappeared into the house. How could she have fallen back into this confrontational relationship with her father? Hadn't Rafiq told her he could only run her life if she let him? It was time to move on.

Suddenly she wished Rafiq was beside her. He understood her—better than anyone ever had.

A wave of gratitude swept her. She'd been fortunate to find a man who suited her perfectly—yet she was far from an ideal wife. Guilt ate at her. Given any choice, Rafiq would never have married her.

She was just as guilty of boxing him into a corner as all the women he'd so smartly evaded. And one day he was going to bitterly resent her for taking away his freedom.

"Looks like your husband will be able to keep you in a style that will be easy to get accustomed to. That's quite a display." Her father's return from where he'd been inspecting an illuminated manuscript in a glass case cut into her thoughts. "But I want to see that I can leave you in this man's care."

Tiffany refrained from telling her father that Rafiq had already saved her from more scrapes than her father ever had. That she loved him. That she wanted to stay by his side for every day of her life. That the last thing her husband needed was an overzealous parent — he'd had enough of those.

The sound of voices led Rafiq to where his wife and her visitors were sitting on the balcony overlooking the desert. He loved this spot in the evenings, when the heat subsided and the desert came to life. He paused on the threshold, drinking in the sight of Tiffany.

She was perched on one of the thickly padded chairs, the center point of the family group. If he hadn't known she was pregnant, the healthy glow of her skin and the sheen of her hair would've given it away. An older woman, who had to be Linda, with salt-and-pepper hair and a kindly face sat beside her, while a thin, bearded man full of nervous energy dominated the conversation.

Rafiq strode forward. All three of them looked up.

A shadow passed over Tiffany's face, then she leaped up. "Rafiq, you're here."

She clung to him, and there was a touch of desperation in the kiss she gave him.

"What's the matter?" he asked.

She shook her head, then let go of him.

Uneasy, he waited.

She introduced her parents with a bright smile, tension evident in every line of her body. Rafiq frowned, trying to fathom what was worrying her. At first he thought her parents might be causing her strain, but he couldn't see any evidence of that. Linda appeared to be doing her best to do everything to ease the situation, while Tiffany's father clearly thought of no one other than himself.

Tiffany caught his eye. "I'd like to talk to you, Rafiq."

Her somber expression caused a dart of concern.

After excusing himself from the company, he followed her down the stairs, along the walkway lined with palms, and onto the edge of the desert beyond. "What's wrong? Are you in pain? Is it the baby?"

The helplessness that he experienced was a first. Rafiq discovered he didn't like it at all.

She shook her head. "It's nothing like that."

But she kept knotting and unknotting her fingers. The gesture didn't reassure Rafiq. "Then what is it?" he demanded. "What's the matter?"

"I've trapped you into this marriage."

His heart stood still. "What?"

"You would never have married me if I hadn't been pregnant. It's just like all those other women who tried to corner you into marriage—except this time there was a baby. You couldn't get out of it. One day you're going to resent me—even the child."

An air of dejection surrounded her.

"That's not just any child. That's my daughter you're talking about."

Tiffany hesitated, then blurted out, "You said 'my daughter.' Do you mean that? Do you believe it? Or are you just saying it to make me feel better?"

"Oh, I mean it."

"And what about being trapped?"

"I'm not trapped."

Tiffany started to shake. "I thought…" She broke off.

"What did you think?"

"I thought that you were going to hate me. That you'd one day feel that I'd tricked you."

"Oh, Tiffany. I was always going to marry you."

"To legitimize the baby—out of duty."

"Because I wanted you. Because I couldn't keep my hands off you." He stepped up beside her and wrapped his arms around her, then rested his chin on her shoulder. "I don't care what your father does in his life, I want you. And nothing, not your father, not my father, is going to keep me from having you."

From her silence he knew that she required some mental adjustment.

So he added for good measure, "If you look behind us, you'll see that your father has just taken your mother's hand. His behavior is her problem—unless they decide to get divorced."

"Do you think she'd take him back? He's a serial adulterer.... He needs to grow up."

"So I've gathered."

"Did I tell you that?"

"You didn't need to." He stroked her hair. "But don't make the mistake of confusing me with your father."

"Oh, I won't," she assured him. "You're nothing like him. My mother is in for a lot more heartache if she takes him back."

"He may have missed her. He may want to change his ways. But don't think his behavior is your responsibility."

"I thought you would think—"

"You think entirely too much!"

She didn't smile. "So who my father is won't make you think any less of me?"

He shook his head. "Just like who your father is won't make me think any more of you, either." Then he started to laugh. "I'm not being totally consistent."

"What do you mean?"

"I told Julian that I had no intention of ever marrying

his daughter because I couldn't be sure she hadn't slept around as much as he has."

She pulled out of his arms, and swiveled to face him. The waning sunlight turned the tips of her lashes to gold. "Julian? You mean Sir Julian Carling?"

He nodded.

"But you can't marry her, you're married to me."

"You noticed," he said smugly.

"Of course I noticed!"

"Good."

He leaned forward and kissed her. He took his time, and did it thoroughly, not caring that her parents might be watching.

When he'd finished, she returned to the subject like a dog with a bone. "Why was Sir Julian talking to you about marrying his daughter?"

"He wasn't talking to me about it. He was discussing it with my father," he said then laughed as she placed her hands on her hips and glared at him. "They had decided I should divorce you and marry Elizabeth Carling."

"Divorce me?" Tiffany's bravado disappeared like a deflated balloon. She looked stunned, then apprehensive.

"Don't worry. I told them that I had no intention of divorcing you—that you were pregnant with my baby. And, yes, I believe that. Just as I believe that you were a virgin that first night we made love." He also knew that this woman would never bore him. She was his forever. "Now it's my turn to make a confession."

"What is it?"

He handed her a piece of paper. "I never did intend to stay married to you after we had the tests done."

"You intended to cut and run if the baby wasn't yours?"

He nodded. "And if it was mine I intended to keep the baby here, divorce you and send you home."

"What an utterly diabolical plot!"

"I know." He pointed to the paper she held. "That contract you're holding will ensure that you will feel safe, that I will never do something like that. You only need to sign it."

She glanced at it, then flung her arms around him. "You know I told myself I was looking for someone ordinary."

"The man that you're looking for is going to be very hard to find."

"No." She released him and shook her head. "I've decided he isn't what I want. I want someone special. Someone like you. No one ordinary would ever have confessed what you did—or given me that kind of assurance in writing. I love you. That's very hard for me to say. I'm beginning to think I never intended to love anyone. But I love you because you are incredibly special."

His heart stopped at her confession. "I love you, too. You are the most important person in my whole world. You fill my world," he whispered, drawing her back into his arms. "There is only you. There will only ever be you."

* * * * *

Silhouette *Desire*

COMING NEXT MONTH
Available November 9, 2010

REQUEST YOUR FREE BOOKS!

**2 FREE NOVELS
PLUS 2
FREE GIFTS!**

Silhouette®

Desire®

Passionate, Powerful, Provocative!

YES! Please send me 2 FREE Silhouette Desire® novels and my 2 FREE gifts (gifts are worth about $10). After receiving them, if I don't wish to receive any more books, I can return the shipping statement marked "cancel." If I don't cancel, I will receive 6 brand-new novels every month and be billed just $4.05 per book in the U.S. or $4.74 per book in Canada. That's a saving of at least 15% off the cover price! It's quite a bargain! Shipping and handling is just 50¢ per book.* I understand that accepting the 2 free books and gifts places me under no obligation to buy anything. I can always return a shipment and cancel at any time. Even if I never buy another book, the two free books and gifts are mine to keep forever.

225/326 SDN E5QG

Name	(PLEASE PRINT)	

Address		Apt. #

City	State/Prov.	Zip/Postal Code

Signature (if under 18, a parent or guardian must sign)

Mail to the Silhouette Reader Service:

IN U.S.A.: P.O. Box 1867, Buffalo, NY 14240-1867
IN CANADA: P.O. Box 609, Fort Erie, Ontario L2A 5X3

Not valid for current subscribers to Silhouette Desire books.

**Want to try two free books from another line?
Call 1-800-873-8635 or visit www.morefreebooks.com.**

* Terms and prices subject to change without notice. Prices do not include applicable taxes. N.Y. residents add applicable sales tax. Canadian residents will be charged applicable provincial taxes and GST. Offer not valid in Quebec. This offer is limited to one order per household. All orders subject to approval. Credit or debit balances in a customer's account(s) may be offset by any other outstanding balance owed by or to the customer. Please allow 4 to 6 weeks for delivery. Offer available while quantities last.

Your Privacy: Silhouette Books is committed to protecting your privacy. Our Privacy Policy is available online at www.eHarlequin.com or upon request from the Reader Service. From time to time we make our lists of customers available to reputable third parties who may have a product or service of interest to you. If you would prefer we not share your name and address, please check here. ☐

Help us get it right—We strive for accurate, respectful and relevant communications. To clarify or modify your communication preferences, visit us at www.ReaderService.com/consumerschoice.

SDES10R

HARLEQUIN®

A *Romance*

FOR EVERY MOOD™

Spotlight on

Inspirational

Wholesome romances
that touch the heart and soul.

See the next page
to enjoy a sneak peek from
the Love Inspired® Suspense
inspirational series.

*See below for a sneak peek from
our inspirational line, Love Inspired® Suspense*

*Enjoy this heart-stopping excerpt from
RUNNING BLIND
by top author Shirlee McCoy,
available November 2010!*

**The mission trip to Mexico was supposed to be an
adventure. But the thrill turns sour when Jenna Dougherty
and her roommate Magdalena are kidnapped.**

"It's okay. I'm here to help." The voice was as deep as the
darkness, but Jenna Dougherty didn't believe the lie. She
could do nothing but lie still as hands slid down her arms,
felt the rope around her wrists.

"I'm going to use a knife to cut you free, Jenna. Hold
still."

The cold blade of a knife pressed close to her head before
her gag fell away.

"I—" she started, but her mouth was dry, and she could
do nothing but suck in air.

"Shhh. Whatever needs to be said can be said when
we're out of here." Nick spoke quietly, his hand gentle on
her cheek. There and gone as he sliced through the ropes on
her wrists and ankles.

He pulled her upright. "Come on. We may be on
borrowed time."

"I can't leave my friend," Jenna rasped out.

"There's no one here. Just us."

"She has to be here." Jenna took a step away.

"There's no one here. Let's go before that changes."

"It's dark. Maybe if we find a light…"

"What did you say?"

"We need to turn on the light. I can't leave until I know that—"

"What can you see, Jenna?"

"Nothing."

"No shadows? No light?"

"No."

"It's broad daylight. There's light spilling in from the window I climbed in through. You can't see it?"

She went cold at his words.

"I can't see anything."

"You've got a nasty bruise on your forehead. Maybe that has something to do with it." His fingers traced the tender flesh on her forehead.

"It doesn't matter *how* it happened. I'm blind!"

Can Nick help Jenna find her friend or will chasing this trail have Jenna running blindly again into danger?

Find out in RUNNING BLIND, available in November 2010 only from Love Inspired Suspense.

OLIVIA GATES

brings you the first alluring story in the new miniseries *Pride of Zohayd*.

TO TAME A SHEIKH

To keep the peace in the state of Zohayd, Shaheen must find a bride. What he didn't expect was to fall for the woman he shared a single night of passion with. Could this be Johara, the daughter of the royal jeweler, the same girl he grew up with?

Johara has loved Shaheen since she was six and he, fourteen. Twelve years later she returns to see him before he's to choose a bride, and she is suddenly suspected of stealing royal jewels.

Will Shaheen trust his heart or save the state?

Available November 9, 2010

Always Powerful, Passionate and Provocative.